AF405658

THE SS EXODUS

Prologue

Doctor Levi Goldschmidt: engineer, scientist, pretty much a genius.

Born into wealth in Stuttgart, Germany, Levi graduated from university with a masters degree in aerospace engineering (with honours), travelled the world, visiting countries including – but not limited to – India, Japan, China and Russia, but eventually settled in Britain to live with his new wife, Samantha.

In the year 2044, Levi Goldschmidt gathered his smartest friends from around the globe to form GASO: the Goldschmidt Aeronautics and Space Organisation, and in the years following, they would plan and found a tiny village, lovingly named Ruhigdorf. Quiet village, as it's name literally translated into German. And there they would all reside with their respective families in a little oasis of peace and of science. But their endeavours didn't come to a halt there.

Soon, they would start planning their biggest project yet: a huge, yet affordable, hotel with a twist: it would orbit the Earth in space. A *space hotel* that would match the expectations set by engineers before them who had promised something similar and never delivered.

And in 2051, they started building.

Doctor Levi Goldschmidt was a workaholic. Having such a large task on the go didn't stop him working on his own, smaller, personal projects at the same time. The village grew in size, and so did his family, although not every member was strictly human.

Mason was the name of a hyper-humanoid android built as part of a competition between Levi and one of his smartest friends. An android race, if you will. Although her completion was a little rushed, Mason became a strong friend of the family, and of GASO in general.

Everything was perfect.

And in the year 2073, that great behemoth of a spacecraft – since dubbed the SS Exodus – was finally complete.

Celebration, tears of joy, tears of laughter. Years of blood sweat and tears had finally paid off.

Everybody was overjoyed, but most overjoyed of all of them was Doctor Levi.

Then he died.

'The Great Fire of '76' spread through the quiet village like a ravenous wolf, swallowing up buildings and trees and, of course, people.

It started out in the forest behind Levi's family's impressively-sized home, but it spread like the Great Fire of London. The bright red flames hid the night sky's stars behind a cloud of black smoke. And by the time it cleared, some of the brightest stars had been snuffed out for good: the great minds who had worked so hard to build the village in the first place.

Ruhigdorf was reduced to ashes, and so were all but thirty of its residents. A tiny fragment of humanity who had nowhere to go but up.

To space.

<u>Chapter 1</u>

Cassiopeia Goldschmidt impatiently tapped her shoe on the white ceramic floor of the lounge. The sound echoed through the empty room, bouncing off the glass, the floor, the walls, and back to Cassiopeia's ears again. She blew out a small, bored sigh and crossed her arms with exasperation.

Cassiopeia – 'Cass' to her friends – was the only one rescued from the burning mess of the Goldschmidt estate. Carried out of the flames in her sleep by none other than Mason, the android her father created. She was eleven years old at the time.

Now she was eighteen and living in space on a huge spacecraft with thirty other people. And she was bored to death.

Mason should have been here ten minutes ago.

The android herself worked below the main floor of the space station, in a little workshop. She had been programmed with an impressively high skill of engineering, and had been designated the job of repairing this and that around the Exodus, including anything that happened to go wrong with the two other androids on board.

Cass shook her fringe out of her face and brushed it back with her fingers to sit to the side like it was meant to. It was something of a mix between a faux hawk and an undercut with longer sides. It was currently way longer and stragglier than Cass liked it, and the pink tips were starting to fade out. She could have gone to get it cut and come back again in the time it was taking Mason to get here.

With another exaggerated sigh, Cass got to her feet and started to make her way out of the lounge. It was a communal lounge, used by the whole station, with a vast window on one wall that looked out onto the stars. Such a view would have been enough to keep any normal person entranced for hours, but Cass had seen it enough by now to start getting bored of it. In the of the room proudly stood a cherry blossom tree made entirely of glass, but apart from this, there was nothing else in the room besides chairs and little coffee tables. Normally, the lounge would be brimming with life as people sat around chatting and having fun, but it was dinner time right now, so there wasn't even anyone to talk to.

Timekeeping was not one of Mason's skills.

Cass stepped into the long concourse outside and gazed along it to where it opened up into a circular atrium-style lobby at the end. Two sets of stairs, one on either side of a small lift, curved up to the mezzanine of the second floor. And just above the lift was a large, digital-display clock emanating a constant ultramarine blue light. Cass always thought it looked like a countdown timer from an old sci-fi film.

The concourse was lined with different amenities, one of which was the café where Cass worked. And another was the pub-restaurant that she and Mason frequented along with their small group of friends. She gazed in through the window as she walked past, but Mason wasn't there.

She must still be 'working'.

Her job wasn't too demanding. It was pretty infrequent that anything needed urgently fixing on the Exodus, so a lot of Mason's work hours were filled with her messing around with little objects and trying to make something useful. And reading. She loved reading.

Eventually, Cass reached the lift and, once its doors had slowly dragged open, she got in and jabbed the minus-one button. The lift wasn't her favourite thing. She didn't like the way it suddenly started moving and she didn't like the way her stomach smacked against her ribs like a wet fish when it stopped.

When she stepped out again, she didn't feel much better. As a passenger, she had a feeling in the back of her mind that she shouldn't be down here. But nobody had ever told her off for it, so she braved the trip down anyway.

The door to the workshop was unlocked as usual so Cass let herself in. She kept her eyes on the floor as she moved through the room, just in case Mason had left something lying around that wouldn't be good to step on, like glass or a shard of metal of some sort. It had been known to happen.

"Mason?" Cass called, not quite at a shout, but a touch higher than speaking volume. When she got no response she repeated slightly louder, *"Mason?"*

She hoped that her friend hadn't got herself in trouble with Jonah, the commander of the Exodus. He ran a tight ship and could be ruthless if angered. And it didn't take much to anger him. Even just glancing at him the wrong way could send him into a fury. But mostly, he kept to himself, up in his cabin, where he'd watch over the Exodus with eagle eyes and creased brow. He was not the friendliest of fellows.

Even worse, he was Cass' uncle.

"Mason!" she called out once more, starting to get concerned. Then she saw.

The operating table at the end of the room would be used for making repairs to the androids on board. The leg and arm parts branched out separately, with straps on each one to secure limbs in place, and the back curved up so that the patient could sit more upright.

The thing made Cass uneasy, but what made her more uneasy was the sight of a body on top of it.

Mason. Arms and legs hanging limply here and there instead of positioned on the chair. The lights hanging in a circle above shone down onto her like a dramatic spotlight in a theatre play and a mess of papers were lying over her torso, with some pages having drifted off onto the floor.

Cass pulled a face and stepped closer, cautiously.

"Mason, if this is some sort of funny-ha-ha prank, you can give it up now," she said gravely, though the nervousness still shone through in her voice, "...Hey. Stop it."

She stood beside the table, looking down at the body, her heart fluttering about with nerves.

Her friend was motionless.

Chapter 2

In the midst of the blaze that struck the Goldschmidt estate all those years ago, Mason had made a beeline to young Cass' bedroom. She lifted up the child in her arms and carried her down the hall as fast as she could. While they did get out safely, half of Mason's face had caught alight in the escape. It melted in sinewy bits like stringy pizza cheese, and after it had been cut away neatly, the whole right half was gone, including the eye. Now you could see the titanium skull that lay beneath, and the one (permanently on) light in the otherwise empty eye socket.

It looked a little eerie. Scared Cass when she was younger, too. But over the years, she'd slowly become used to it.

"Lights are on. Nobody's home," she sighed, putting a hand on her shoulder.

Mason's one good eye shot open and Cass retracted her hand as if she'd been burnt.

"What's wrong, why are you clutching your heart like that?" Mason asked in her usual flat tone.

"You scared the life out of me!" Cass whined, "I thought you were dead or something."

"Dead? I don't think so... I must have dropped off whilst reading."

Since her facial injury, Mason occasionally experienced little glitches and errors, such as going into 'standby' mode accidentally, or becoming stuck in a vocal loop for a few seconds. Usually, these things didn't really impact her life on a major scale, but it was times like these that they were inconvenient.

"You're late for dinner," Cass sighed, sliding her hands into her pockets, as Mason went about gathering up the papers that had fallen onto the floor, "You want to head up to the pub?"

"Sure. Sorry to keep you waiting, Cass."

The pub's full name was actually the 'Exodus Pub', but since it was a given that it was on the Exodus – and the *only* one on it, too – everyone simply called it 'the pub'. It was modelled after an old English bar but with the added modern touch of a few neon lights here and there. The place's signature drink was the 'constellation cocktail', which was a mix of vodka, coffee liquor, grenadine, syrup and chocolate sauce, topped with grated chocolate. Cass had tried it once and decided that the best word for it was 'dreadful'.

Despite the questionable drinks, the two still enjoyed visiting the establishment, mostly thanks to the entertainment.

At twelve midday, seven in the evening and at midnight, the little stage in the corner would be occupied with the talent of the ship's resident performers, Leo and Orion.

As it happened, Leo was the creation of Levi's friend, Dr Hiroshi Hatsumi. Leo was the *other* outcome of the android-building race, and

when he was completed, he was sent to live with
an old house-bound pianist until his death in the
Ruhigdorf fire. Now, Leo sang onstage with his
closest friend, Orion. And he had a grand voice,
too.

Accompanying his voice was the sharp yet
classy sound of Orion's electric violin, which
could be heard, muffled, from outside the pub as
Cass and Mason approached.

As they entered, that familiar pungent smell
of old spilled beer hit them. They took a seat at
their favourite table facing the stage. The floor was
a bit tacky and the thin drinks coasters were stuck
to the tables, but it was comfortable.

Orion flashed a glance at them from his
place on the stage before he went into a frankly
very impressive violin solo. Mason had no doubt
he was annoyed that she had missed the beginning
of the performance.

"So what were you reading earlier?" Cass
asked, breaking the silence at last.

"Oh, just some blueprints of the ship.
Nothing much."

"No wonder you fell asleep, that sounds
worse than watching paint dry."

"It wasn't so bad," Mason shrugged, fixing
her hair with one hand while she rested the other
on the table. She eyed the approaching waitress
from the corner of her eye as the violin solo played
to a close.

"Can I take your order?" asked the waitress, teeth sticking to the chewing gum in her mouth as she spoke. She regularly served Mason and Cass, and wasn't afraid to barge in in the middle of a conversation. Mason had also never seen her open her eyes more than halfway.

Mason herself, despite being impressively human, could not eat a thing. If she attempted to, in some ill-conceived experiment, anything solid would get stuck in her throat, or otherwise jam up her systems. And nobody wants to deal with jammed up systems. Instead, the androids could consume liquids, which wouldn't clog up anything. Soup, too, if it was smooth enough. Mason's favourite was coffee.

"Double espresso, if you would, please," she asked, politely. Caffeine did not affect her in the slightest and she couldn't even taste it, but she very much enjoyed holding the tiny cup and saucer in her hand.

"And I'll have the usual," Cass added, and the waitress drifted off into the kitchen without another word.

Mason leaned back in her chair and folded her arms, looking down at Cass with an air of exasperation.

"It wouldn't kill you to order something else every once in a while."

"Says you with your double espresso."

"This is the twentieth day in a row you've ordered pepperoni pizza. Yes, I am counting."

"It's my *routine,*" Cass insisted, "It's not like I'm going to die from pepperoni overdose. You know, sometimes I think you really believe you're my mother."

Mason had no comeback for this one, so she turned away with a *'tch…'.* She was technically Cass' guardian, since Levi's untimely demise, and admittedly she did occasionally start trying too hard to be a parent.

As she was trying to formulate some sort of response, a round of applause reverberated around the room. When she realised that the clapping was to mark the end of Leo and Orion's performance, and not to celebrate Cass' argumentative victory, she joined in, too.

Both Leo and Orion took a short bow for the little crowd and then slipped backstage through the red velvet curtain. They reappeared moments later and began to make their way over to the table.

In terms of physical appearance, Orion and Leo were quite the opposite of each-other. Orion had a soft, gentle face with dimples and faintly rosy cheeks. His hair was deep red, styled into a side-swept fringe that fell down to his temples, and his sympathetic eyes had dark patches in the corners. He looked warm, he looked kind, and his voice was mellow and tired.

On the other hand, Leo stood tall and lissom. Everything about him was slim and pointy. Long legs, long neck, long face. His eyes were slender, his cheekbones high, and upon his defined nose perched a pair of round, rose-gold glasses. He did not require these to see, but rather he wore them as a statement piece.

Both men pulled back their chairs and took a seat at the table in perfect synchrony.

"You missed the start of our show," Orion said. He sounded slightly thwarted, but not shocked, "...Again."

"Sorry," Mason apologised, "I… got distracted."

But Leo swung an arm around her shoulder and told her not to worry about it.

"There's always tonight!" he smiled before swiftly whisking his arm away. He hurried to compose himself, flicking the long wave of black hair that flowed to the left of his face out of the way – it was always falling in front of his eyes and he was constantly fixing it – and straightening his waistcoat, "Uh, Orion and I don't have any plans for later on, so if you two want to come over and catch up, that would be… I mean, if that's alright with you and you're free and everything… but if you don't want to, that's okay too."

Cass gave him a reassuring smile.

"We'll be there," she nodded.

"We'll have to tidy up first," Orion added, rolling up his white shirt sleeves, slowly and methodically, "The place is a mess. Pens everywhere."

"I was organising," Leo frowned, "It's my collection."

"Your *hoard,* more like-"

But Orion's complaining was interrupted by an arm in front of his face as the waitress returned. He sat up straighter in his seat to look over the intruding arm across at Mason,

"I opened the cutlery drawer earlier to get a spoon and there was a fountain pen in-amongst the sporks," he grumbled, and Cass giggled at his quandary before taking a long sip of cola.

Mason neatly turned around her espresso cup so that the handle was on the right side and, self-satisfied, clasped her hands together.

"Look at this. The perfect espresso. With just the right amount of foam; that's got to be at least a centimetre of just foam."

"I'd say one and a half," Leo put in.

"One and a half, even!"

"It is the perfect espresso."

But from the way that her face fell back to neutral when Leo looked away, Cass could tell that something was weighing on Mason's mind.

"...Hey, is everything alright?" she quietly inquired, leaning her elbows on the table.

Mason's good eye reeled around to follow her movement.

"Well. There was one… small thing."

"Go on?"

"It's about the supply plane."

<u>Chapter 3</u>

"What about the supply plane?"

"Well. I just noticed that it hadn't docked yesterday like it usually does. That's all."

"Was that meant to be yesterday?"

Orion's tone was soft, tired, and seemingly unconcerned. He folded his arms and leaned back in his chair to rest his eyes a moment.

"I'm sure it's nothing. Maybe 'Commander Jonah' up there gave them the wrong date by mistake."

"Jonah's usually very punctual," Mason pointed out, "I don't think he would have given them an incorrect date. Besides, it's always every sixty days, they could work it out."

She was right. Every sixty days, GASO would dispatch a space plane to deliver necessities to the Exodus. And it was always exactly on time.

Mason shifted her gaze momentarily to watch Cass poke around in the cola glass with her paper straw. She didn't make eye contact, just kept her sights trained on the glass.

Realising her choice in conversation may have rattled Cass' mood a bit, Mason quickly returned to talking with Orion and Leo.

"You're right. It's probably nothing."

"It's not like we're going to run out of food or anything," Leo put in with a shrug and a smile, before leaning over to Orion and whispering, *"We won't run out of food, will we?"*

Orion shook his head, eyes still closed.

'Not that it would matter to you,' he thought.

"Just me being paranoid," Mason nodded, "I'm sure it'll be here soon. A hold-up down on Earth, perhaps." and she laid the matter to rest for now. Maybe, she thought, she should have brought it up when Cass wasn't around.

After a few moments of silence, Cass finally raised her head, looking up at Leo.

"Leo. Can you tell us a story?"

"A story?"

"Yeah. About your life before you came to live here. You always have fun little stories."

"Huh… Well, I suppose so. Let me think…"

Here he paused a second, absent-mindedly rubbing his hands together and blowing out a low whistle. Eventually he seemed to experience a thought.

"Ah, I know," he started, "It was a long time ago, when I'd just started living with old Alexander. I think I'd been there a few months at most."

The others settled down to listen patiently.

"Alexander had sent me out on a regular errand. A run down to the bakery to pick up some bread. They were baked fresh in the morning, see, and if I got there early enough I'd be able to get them home while they were still warm. *Very* early, mind you. There was still dew in the air from the

rain the night before and there was hardly a soul
around. And as I was walking along the pathway,
do you know, I heard something."

He looked momentarily to everybody's
faces in turn to check that they were listening and
were well and truly interested before continuing
his tale,

"It sounded like a little mewing. So I
looked around to see where it was coming from,
and behind a recycling bin I saw this tiny shape. A
kitten! So small and shaky and, I assumed, alone.
Well, I couldn't just leave him there. So I picked
him up and carried him in my arms to the bakery.
And when I got there, I said to the baker, 'do you
know whose cat this is?' and the baker said 'no, I
don't, I'm afraid'. So I thought, well, if it is
someone's cat, they'll go looking for it at some
point, so if I look after it for until they do, they'll
find him safe and sound with me.

So I bought the bread, all wrapped up in a
paper bag, and I tucked it into the bottom of my
satchel, and I let the kitten lie on top so he was
warm, and I took him home. I called him Basil
because the bread in question was tomato basil,
and Tomato didn't seem like a very good name.
And I wrapped him in a blanket and fed him and
kept him a secret. Alexander didn't like cats, you
see. He didn't like any pets."

"Did you get to keep him?" Cass asked.

"Oh, no. Though I wanted to. Alexander
found out about him after a few weeks when he

noticed I was buying a lot of canned tuna. I admit I could have been more tactful with my choice in feed, being that Alexander didn't actually like canned tuna. But what's done is done. No, I had to give little Basil over to an animal rescue centre. The closest one was some distance away, so someone from the village had to take him there. Basil and I had an emotional goodbye. I hope he's doing well now, wherever he happens to be. It was for the best, really, considering… well. That's a lot of responsibility, I mean."

"Maybe you can get another cat, now you don't live with Alexander any more."

"A cat on the Exodus? What a thought. I don't think Jonah would have it."

"He denied my request for a goldfish," Orion said, clearly still a little upset over the matter.

"I'd let you have a goldfish if I was in charge," Cass assured him.

"I'd put you in charge in place of Jonah any day of the week," Leo said.

"I think we all would," Orion seconded. There weren't many people on board the Exodus who liked Jonah, and there weren't many people who Jonah liked, either. In fact, the last time he came down to the main floor of the ship, he made a huge scene because the server at the café made his tea wrong. The server took it well, though, and the comedic, pedantic order of Earl Grey with 'exactly two teaspoons of milk' had become a bit of a running joke amongst the staff since.

Swiftly, Leo got to his feet. He brushed himself down and neatened his sleeves, standing tall and composed,

"I'm afraid I must leave you now," he announced, "I have a flat to clean in preparation for your visit later," and he smiled, flashing sharp fangs, before taking an extravagant bow and turning to leave.

Orion rolled his eyes at his friend's over-the-top departure and slowly got up to follow him, with a low "See you later," as he went.

And with that, Mason and Cass were abruptly left alone once more. In silence.

Cass took a long, drawn-out sip of her drink.

"Mason. About the supply plane. You really think it's nothing? They haven't forgotten or anything?"

"It'll be here sometime."

"...What *would* happen if we ran out of food, Mason?"

"Then I'd make sure we were the last ones standing, and I'd save all the food I found for you," Mason said with a motherly smile.

"And Orion?"

"Yes, we'd save some for Orion, too."

<u>Chapter 4</u>

Orion and Leo's cabin was in complete and utter disarray.

Sheet music, pens, chocolate wrappers and socks were scattered around the place from their mad rush to get out of the door earlier in time for their performance. It wasn't usually this bad, but Orion hadn't had time for dinner and had had to fix a couple of notes of his song before they got out of the door, struggling in the process to find one of Leo's pens that still had ink left.

Taking care not to stand on anything as he entered, Leo bent down to gather some papers from the floor. Ahead of him, he heard Orion place his violin case down on his bed with an exhausted sigh, followed by a strained groan as he stretched out his arms.

Straightening up and placing the papers in a neat pile on the sideboard, Leo took a long gaze around the room he shared with his friend. Originally, they'd had a room each when they first moved onto the ship, but since they visited each other so regularly, they eventually opted to share. The cabin was practically identical to every other twin room on the ship. It wasn't especially huge, but it definitely wasn't small either. Two single beds were lined up against the wall with a divider between them, patterned with stars. And opposite the door, against the window, a table and two chairs faced out of the window, out into the abyss.

Sometimes if you leaned around you could see the Earth below, just floating there in the oily-black sky.

Apart from that, there was just the typical hotel-room amenities; wardrobes, cabinets, a bookshelf, large screen upon the wall, a small kitchenette and a full bathroom right off the side. It was more a studio apartment than a hotel room. And it was *usually* kept very neat, too. Especially since there would be routine room inspections every so often, and nobody wanted to be caught not taking proper care of their allotted space, or else be punished with a stern word.

Conveniently, they lived next door to Mason. In fact, Leo and Mason's first meeting was when they were both leaving their rooms. Leo remembered it vividly…

"Oh! Good morning, miss! Sorry, I didn't see you there," he had grinned, awkwardly, after almost walking straight into her. And she had turned around to look up at him, and the look of her face had taken him quite by surprise. Despite the missing half of her face and the open eye socket, Leo regarded her as quite stunning. The contrast of deep black hair against paper pale skin, the one vibrant emerald eye, the smart suit. It was all quite eye-catching.

"Hey," she had responded, flatly but not rudely. Or, at least, Leo hoped it wasn't meant to be rude.

"I'm Leo, I live just next door. I don't believe we've met?"

"Oh, that Leo?"

"...I don't know, am I 'that' Leo?"

"I heard Doctor Goldschmidt mention a 'Leo' a few times. Do you know a Doctor Hatsumi?"

"Oh, you must be Mason! Hatsumi is my creator, he said many wonderful things about the Goldschmidt family. I wonder how it's been this long and we haven't met."

Mason shrugged in a sort of 'why are you asking me?' sort of manner. She seemed altogether unexcited by the exchange, but generally happy to be talking to someone.

"I'd stay and chat, but I'm already late for work. I'll see you around, Leo," she told him before either of them could come up with any advance to the conversation.

"Sure! I mean-... no, that is what I mean. I'll see you around, too, Mason."

They'd shaken hands briefly before Mason went on her way. And Leo had been left standing there with nothing behind his eyes, having completely forgotten what he was supposed to be doing.

"Leo? Hey? Are you with us?"

Leo was pulled back to the present by the voice of his room-mate, who was giving him quite the worried look.

"I'm here."

"Oh, good. Thought you'd started… malfunctioning or something."

"Me? Never. This is quality engineering right here," Leo smiled, taking a bow and gesturing vaguely to himself.

"Right…" Orion's eyebrow bent in a dubious grimace. Leo's voice box had been known to encounter the odd error every now and then. Usually it only occurred when he strained it to a note that was either too high or – more often – too low. His voice would be mangled into a mess of bass and treble, unable to produce a comprehensible word. Then he'd have to get Mason to fiddle around until he could speak again. Sometimes Orion wondered whether his friend purposefully broke his voice just to spend some time with Mason. It wouldn't shock him.

"Are you going to help me clean up?"

"Of course, of course…"

"We can watch a movie afterwards, I'll let you choose."

Leo's eyes immediately lit up in excitement at the very prospect.

"You want to watch *Grease* again, don't you?" Orion sighed, but Leo only shrugged and smiled in return.

"It's a classic."

Chapter 5

"*Another* theory? You're rolling these things out like some kind of… conspiracy factory."

"Hear me out this time. It's about the fire."

"...The fire? We already know who started the fire, it was that, uh… that Kay dude."

"But what if it *wasn't* him?"

Mason stopped in her tracks and casually clasped her hands behind her back. The discussion to her left had piqued her interest, but she feared they might go silent if they knew she was listening.

"Who is it, then? Go on, elaborate."

"This is going to sound absolutely wild, but I reckon it was Jonah."

There was silence for a second as the other person, a woman with dark hair and some frankly very impressive cat-eye spectacles, studied the face of her conversational companion, trying to figure out if he was joking or not.

"You're right, that does sound wild," she said eventually.

"Think about it!" the man scrambled to continue his argument, but as he looked up he caught sight of Mason over his friend's shoulder and paused mid-sentence.

Mason hadn't even realised she'd been staring. She gave them a nod to say hello and awkwardly went on her way to the stairs. She didn't really want to hear the end of that conversation anyway.

She didn't talk much to the residents of the ship besides her friend group unless she had to, and they never really approached her either. But she knew them all by vague acquaintance.

After the fire of Ruhigdorf, the survivors had evacuated the village to gather at Jonah's house a mile or so away. It was a grand house, set in the middle of a field with a massive driveway and five bedrooms, which he had no use for as he lived alone aside from his butler, Felix. He had been persuaded to house a few families for a while, and the others went to stay in the nearest hotels or with family until it was decided that they would move onto the Exodus. Mason had stayed at Jonah's house with Cass and had become, not quite friends, but acquaintances with the others who stayed there.

She'd never been keen on Jonah either, but she had never considered him to be the arsonist sort.

She stepped up onto the third floor of the Exodus where the rooms were situated. And if you were to loop back on yourself here, you would see two parallel corridors, one side for even numbers and the other side for odds. Mason took the left corridor on her way. There was a plush white runner laid out all the way down, over the shiny polished floor, and the walls were a sleek light wood panel. In the air was the sharp citrus tang of cleaning fluids, but entirely lacking a sense of smell, this was something Mason had never taken note of.

She stopped in front of room number twenty-seven. The rest of the corridor was silent besides the sound of her friends talking inside. She gave a brisk knock and leaned back on the glass railing behind her as she heard the voices inside soften.

There was a little bleep as the door unlocked and Mason was greeted by Orion's warm face.

"Hi," he smiled, softly, "No Cass?"

"She said she's going to be finishing work late today, the café was busy. She shouldn't be more than… a quarter of an hour?"

"Oh, no problem, then. Come on, come in, we were just having a game of chess."

Mason stepped inside and, sure enough, the chess board was set out on the table beside the window, and in one of the chairs sat Leo, wistfully gazing out into the stars. He looked away when he heard Mason enter and turned to her with a glint in his eye.

"Mason!"

He rose and made an elegant bow before gesturing for Mason to sit opposite him.

"It was a spectacular game," he said, proudly, as he flourished his hands in front of the chess board, "But the black king prevailed once more."

"I think Hatsumi programmed you with some sort of chess-winning code," Orion sighed, folding his arms, "This can't be fair."

"I think you just need to get good," Leo replied.

Orion rolled his eyes and dramatically trudged over to the coffee machine on the kitchen counter to brew a drink.

"Go on, I'll play against you," Mason said with a slight smile, "If you being an android gives you an unjust advantage over Orion, then this should be a fair fight." And she went about setting the pieces out in their starting positions.

She'd played a few games of chess in the past and she'd even attempted three-player circular chess against Levi and Sam, but nobody had won that one because there had been so much disagreement regarding the way the rules worked. The board had been put away somewhere in the attic and had never been pulled out again, which was definitely for the best.

She made her first move as another knock came at the door. Clearly, Cass wasn't as late as she said she would be after all.

Mason and Leo left Orion to greet Cass while they focused on their increasingly more intense chess game. But Mason found her mind drifting elsewhere.

The pieces wobbled sightly as Leo crossed his arms on the table and leaned in to whisper.

"Something's bothering you, isn't it?"

Mason met his sharp, knowing gaze, and wondered how he could tell.

"Maybe… It's nothing, don't worry about it."

"Tell me. It's about the supply plane. Right?"

"…Yes. How can you tell?"

"I just can. Tell me about it."

Mason huffed an animatronic sigh and closed her one good eye. She had to talk quietly, lest Cass overhear. Dearest, sweet Cass, who worried exceedingly over just about anything that presented a threat to the comfort of her daily routine.

"Felix came by earlier, to get one of his hands fixed up. I asked him if he knew anything about the delay and he did that face that he always does when he's trying to think of a good response to a bad question."

"What face is that?" Leo interrupted.

Mason did her best to replicate the expression, an uncomfortable mix of strained and nervous.

Leo nodded his head in understanding,

"I know the one. Continue."

"Well, he looked like that, and then he told me it was nothing for me to worry about. But I thought… if it really was nothing, why didn't he give me a proper explanation? So I thought maybe he was trying to hide something. But maybe I'm just overthinking it."

Leo bit his lip with pointed fangs before finally backing off and sitting back in his chair.

"That's weird. But you know Felix. He always dodges questions like that."

"This was different."

"...I believe you. Look, I know you don't want anyone else to worry about it, but… I want to help investigate. I think that there's something going on but I think that we can get to the bottom of it. Together."

"What are we going to do, then?"

Leo scoffed and shrugged his shoulders, "We'll think of something. Trust me."

Mason decided against bringing up the topic of the man in the lobby's wild accusations.

<u>Chapter 6</u>

If Mason had been human, her work day would have been agony. It wasn't often that there would actually be any work *to* do, and if there was, it usually wouldn't take too long to complete anyway. Mason was quite skilled at her job, given that engineering was one of her core skills, along with basic childcare and rock identification… for some reason. As it was, she didn't really get bored very much. If nothing was happening, she would simply stop thinking for a while and conserve some power until something interesting took place.

This afternoon, heading back from lunch break, Mason would spice up her day by trying something new.

The man behind the counter at the pub looked across at her with a tired stare over the top of his glasses.

"Sorry… we're all out of coffee."

"All out?"

"Yeah, the café is running out too."

"In that case." Mason gave a small smile, "I'll try a tea. To go."

The tea came in a disposable cup with a little logo on the side for the Exodus – a little silhouette of the station with a ring around it, adorned with the words 'Space Station Exodus', and then the same again underneath but in German.

As she left the pub, Mason took a sip of her tea. And it tasted exactly the same as the coffee.

Well, technically, it didn't taste of anything, Mason didn't have taste receptors. So it was, to her, the exact same thing. But something about it was decidedly less exciting. Perhaps hoping for something interesting to happen was a bad idea.

It had been four days since her evening at Leo and Orion's. Four days since she'd become aware of the absence of the supply plane, and she'd almost begun to forget about it. Almost.

Walking down to the basement where she would reside until the end of her shift, she wondered once more what the reason was behind the hold-up.

The coffee drought, she was sure, was simply a co-incidence.

She flicked the desk light on so she didn't have to see solely from the glow of her own eyes, and placed the tea down beside it. She didn't know what she'd been expecting, but the drink still managed to disappoint her.

She slipped off her blazer and draped it over the operating table before moving over to pick up a large book on the shelf behind the desk. The shelf was full of books about robotics and programming and other such subjects – not that Mason needed them, but they spiced up the place – interrupted here and there by the odd fiction novel or true-crime tome. But this particular book was a photo album. Quite the rarity in this day and age.

The cover and back were dark leather, bound at the spine and it was held closed with a long sliver of leather tied in a knot. It was one of the few things that had survived the fire, since it had been kept in a big leather chest at the end of Levi and Samantha's bed. Levi had told Mason about it, long ago.

'If anything happens to me or Sam,' he'd told her, 'You make sure Cass gets this book.'

Sam and Levi had been documenting the Goldschmidt family history, and the various innovative landmarks they had achieved. There was a picture of the Exodus the day it was completed in here somewhere. Mason liked to look through it sometimes. She still hadn't got around to giving it to Cass; somehow she couldn't bring herself to. Maybe it was the fear of bringing up painful memories of times they could never go back to. In any case, she was waiting for the right time, that's what she told herself.

She opened to a random page and studied her own face in the picture. Back when she had all her face. She was there with a young Cass – not older than three or four– helping her onto the back of a Shetland pony. Levi must have taken that photo, since Sam became sick around that time. Samantha passed away after a lengthy struggle with motor neurone disease when Cass was only four. It had knocked everyone in GASO, not only the family. That was when Mason had assumed Sam's mantle of caring for Cass.

She doubted Cass remembered that day, out in the cold and the mud on horseback. But Mason remembered it quite vividly. It was the first and only time she'd ever been to the stables. They were just a little way out of Ruhigdorf, a short car ride or a walk if the weather was nice. Mason hadn't ridden that day, though she had been offered the chance. In all honesty, she was a little afraid to. She wished she had taken the opportunity now.

The stable was fine when the fire broke out, being just out of reach in the moors. That was one good thing at least.

Mason hoped she could go back there one day.

...What was she thinking? Of course she'd get to go back. Soon enough, Ruhigdorf would be fully rebuilt (it was almost there already) and everyone on the Exodus would board a transit plane and fly back to return to their homes and their jobs and their horse riding... Why she'd doubted that even for a moment was beyond her.

She took one last look at the photo, longingly, and moved a hand to the left side of her face where the metal skull underneath was exposed. It wasn't just a scar, it was a grim reminder of everything that was lost that day. A reminder that, despite her best efforts, she couldn't even save one family…

"I hope I'm not interrupting anything?"

Mason moved with such a start her fingers almost slipped through a gap in her face. But she recognised the low, rich voice and quickly regained composure.

"Leo..." she spun around on the saddle stool to face him, "What ails you? Is it the voice again?"

Leo looked a little nervous, perhaps just concerned for the shock he seemed to have caused.

"Oh, nothing like that," he replied, hands clasped together tightly, "I've just been… thinking."

Slowly, Mason crossed her legs.

"Go on?"

Leo was quiet.

"No, I've changed my mind. It's silly. Never mind."

"No, go on, you're here now."

"...Well, I was talking to Tomas, and-"

"Tomas... the theorist?"

"Yes, that one. Look, I know it sounds ridiculous but he brought up a good point about Jonah and about the fire and… well, I was just thinking maybe it could have a connection to what's going on here with the supply plane and everything."

"Is this the rumour about Jonah being an arsonist?"

"He told it to you, too?"

"I overheard. Leo, you know better than to believe everything you hear. Especially from Tomas."

"I know… I know. I'm just getting worried and stressed. People were talking at the pub today, I overheard the staff. They're running low on all sorts of stuff and they can't get any more because there just isn't any, but they're not rationing food or anything, everyone's just going to eat until there's nothing left and then what are we going to do-"

"Overthinking isn't going to help. You should go and calm down. Read a book or watch that one movie you like, just take your mind off it. We'll talk later, alright? I'll meet you in the lounge tonight."

"Alright," Leo nodded, looking like he would have been pouring with sweat if he had the glands for it, "...Sorry for interrupting you. I'll get going."

He turned to leave, but his hand lingered on the door handle. Reluctantly, he gazed back over his shoulder.

"Mason… Tell me it's going to be okay."

Mason's face softened.

"It'll be okay." Her left eye flickered as she gave a thumbs up, "I promise."

Chapter 7

That night, as she had promised, Mason made her way to the lounge at the end of the Exodus. The whole place was barren of people, who had since retired to bed. Apart from a couple of late-night patrons at the pub, which was open 24/7, its dim lights still shining through the windows.

Meeting when no people were around was important; the last thing you want on a space station is panic spreading.

As she entered the lounge, Mason could see Leo seated on one of the sofas beside the window, staring absently into space. He looked back over his shoulder when he heard footsteps approaching and stood up abruptly, but quickly sat back down again.

Mason took a seat beside him without a word. In no rush, as usual.

"So. What's up?"

Leo stared across at her, a little dumbstruck.

"What do you mean 'what's up'? We're running out of food."

"It'll be fine," Mason shrugged. She turned away and casually draped her arm over the back of the couch.

"Stop pretending you don't care!" Leo threw back, smacking his fists down on his lap in frustration.

Mason's eye snapped to look him in the face, watching him calm himself with a long, drawn-out sigh until he was composed once more.

"Sorry," he said, "I don't like the way my voice echoed when I said that."

The room was silent for a while. The only sound being the gentle whirring of both the androids' systems.

Mason had told herself four days ago that the rumour of Jonah igniting the Ruhigdorf fire was simply another of Tomas' unfounded theses. She had a feeling Leo wasn't of the same opinion.

"You really think Jonah is doing something dodgy?"

"Well, I…. I don't know. Maybe. Doesn't he seem the sort?"

"A pyromaniac?"

"A maniac at least. The only time I see him, he's having some sort of meltdown. You're basically part of the Goldschmidt family, what do you know about him?"

"Surprisingly little. The only time I've spoken to him was back in his house when he was hosting us after the fire. He did seem a little… short-tempered. But I assumed that was due to having so many people in his home. And the fact his brother just died."

"How about before that? Did he ever visit Levi and Samantha?"

Mason paused before giving an answer, hearing footsteps and a small voice getting slightly closer. She looked over her shoulder to see who it might be, wondering whether it might be Cass searching for her, or Orion on the hunt for Leo. But she didn't see either of them.

What she saw was the small figure of Felix.

Felix wasn't just Jonah's butler, he was his eyes and ears around the whole of the Exodus. Or, rather, *eye* and ears. Felix was, for want of a better word, an oddity.

Commissioned by Jonah and created by Levi, he was designed to do his job as efficiently as possible, at the cost of a conventional appearance.

The large, singular eye on his face was, in fact, a camera lens. Whatever he saw (and heard) was streamed back to Jonah in real-time. When he had commissioned Felix, Jonah said that the camera was for 'security purposes' around his extensive property. Now it was used to monitor the residents of the SS Exodus.

What Felix lacked in the eye department, he more than made up for in arms, of which he had four. For multi-tasking, it was said. The secondary pair sat a little further back behind his shoulders, and if he held them straight down, you'd never be able to tell they were there.

This extra pair of hands would usually be engaged in anxious fiddling while Felix did other things, and that's exactly what he was doing now. One hand cupped his ear, another one clutching a tablet, and the last two nervously rubbing together.

"Yes… All in order, yes, sir…" he said, voice echoing down the empty concourse, "Well, there was one thing. About those rumours, sir-… yes, I know, but they do seem to be spreading."

He winced in reaction to the harsh voice that came through his earpiece.

"Well, there's nobody around, sir," he continued, lowering his voice and glancing around until he caught sight of Mason and Leo on the couch and quickly looked away, "...Okay, I'll meet you in your cabin in a moment."

His brogue shoes tip-tapped away on the floor as he left.

Slowly, Mason turned back to face Leo again. She was met with his wide-eyed stare, sharp green eyes drilling into her.

"...What?"

"Did that not sound suspicious to you?" Leo hissed, gaze darting back to where Felix was stood for a second as if to point with his eyes.

Deciding to admit defeat at last, Mason droned a mechanical 'sigh'.

"Fine. You were right. But what are we supposed to do about it? Go and confront Jonah?"

Leo winced at the very mention of confrontation.

"What's the other option?"

"I am yet to think of one," Mason replied, flatly.

"Eavesdropping?"

"Have you got a death wish or something?"

"Maybe not, then."

"We're going to have to talk to him. Or, rather, I am. It's up to you if you want to join me."

"When?"

"Tomorrow, probably."

Mason got to her feet, brushing herself down as she did. Despite having one as a butler, Jonah wasn't particularly fond of androids. At least, he wasn't fond of them questioning his authority. Mason wasn't even sure of what she was going to say to him, but she had a while to think about it.

As she turned her back to walk away, she heard Leo get to his feet behind her.

"Mason."

Leo's voice reverberated in the barren room, low and mildly dour,

"...I admire your confidence. I hope you know that."

Mason thought for a while about what an appropriate response to this compliment would be.

"Thank you. I admire your..." she paused, squinting as she thought, "...Glasses."

And although he lacked the embarrassing ability to blush, Leo flashed back a bashful smile.

*

Ever since her mother's death, Cass had been an artist. She sketched out faces, painted memories and collaged together echoes of the past through mementoes and collected odds and ends.

It was Mason who had first posed the idea to her, after having read that creativity was a good way for children to express their emotions. While she wasn't much of an artist herself – she didn't have the imagination for it – Mason had always been her benevolent supporter.

She'd completed an impressive number of artworks in her time on the Exodus, and thus there were canvases both big and small propped up around the room against almost every wall.

Tonight, she was finishing up a small canvas painting, propped up on a tabletop easel. The image was, like most every other painting, a scene from back home.

A quiet electronic beep from behind her signalled the door unlocking, soon followed by its opening and subsequent closing.

"Where've you been?" Cass asked, without turning around.

"Just… with Leo," Mason replied, stiffly, as she took off her shoes.

Cass cracked a smirk,

"With Leo, huh?"

"Why do you sound so… smug?"

"No reason… What were you talking about, then?"

"Not much," Mason responded as she hung up her jacket, but this response didn't seem to convince Cass. Before the interrogation could get into full swing, Mason shifted the conversation to the work in progress on the easel, "Is that the playground behind the house?"

Cass nodded, placing her brush gently into the water jar on her desk.

Behind the Goldschmidt estate was a small wooded area, and a little way into the trees there was a clearing where a tiny playground was positioned. A metal slide, swing set and a wooden climbing frame. After Sam's death, and while Levi was working, Mason would take Cass out there a lot and let her run around while she sat and read a book. Quiet, peaceful, out of the stuffy house.

Levi had become even more of a workaholic than usual after Sam died, so Mason and Cass ended up spending a lot of time together.

"Do you remember the time I nearly went all the way around on the swing?" Cass asked, gazing absently at the swing set in her painting.

"I do," Mason nodded, "For a second I thought you'd fall and break your legs. I panicked a bit."

"Can't imagine you panicking. Doesn't suit you, Mason."

"I save it for strictly necessary situations."

She turned about to the kitchenette to make herself an espresso in their little coffee machine, like she did every night. A part of her wondered whether this was the right time to bring up the photo album, but she was cut off before she could even begin.

"When do you think we're going home, Mason?"

Mason paused, leaning back on the counter and folding her arms.

"I don't know. Can't be long now. Why?"

"Just missing it, that's all. I'd like to be able to go back for good, you know? I'd like to go to an art gallery someday."

"Mm," she hummed with a nod, "I think I'd like to be able to go to a proper coffee shop."

"With Leo?"

"Don't count on it."

Chapter 8

"Good morning! I've come to perform the monthly room inspection courtesy of Commander Goldschmidt. May I come inside?"

Rubbing sleep out of his eyes, having been interrupted from an extremely vivid dream, Orion gazed down upon the expectant face of Felix, standing there with one pair of hands clasped behind his back and the other grasping a tablet and stylus, clipboard-style.

"It's half past six in the morning."

"Apologies for the rude awakening, Mr Sauer. We need to get the inspections out of the way before we go about our day, I'm afraid."

Felix's single mechanical eye twitched and he nervously fixed his cufflinks.

"Fine," Orion sighed, "Come in."

"Thank you."

While other residents of the Exodus would stick to their best behaviour when Felix was around, Orion kept his dislike of Jonah no secret. If Jonah wanted to come down and smack him upside the head for his attitude, Orion thought, so be it. He wasn't on the best terms with Felix, either. The four-armed android gave him the creeps whenever he was around.

Unlike Leo, who had a very definite personality, Felix was – as far as Orion was concerned – a drone. Felix never went to the pub. Felix never went to the coffee shop. He never

49

made small talk with the others, never asked Cass how her art was going, never complimented Leo on his singing. As far as Orion knew, the only person who Felix would talk to besides Jonah was Mason. Maybe it was a family thing.

"Have you been having any problems with your accommodation recently?" Felix inquired, clearly rattling off the same script he'd recited a hundred times before.

"No, it's fine."

"Very good."

Felix ran a gloved finger across the bookshelf and it came away grey and sandy from dust. Discreetly, he wiped it on his trousers. He then went about examining the seal around the window, the electricity sockets and the light fixings before opening a cabinet above the kitchenette to check the hinges and having a small collection of fountain pens spill out onto the counter top and promptly onto the floor. He looked over at Orion with a sad, disappointed gaze.

Clearly, Leo's rushed clean-up last night in preparation for the inspection had not been as careful or as organised as it could have been.

"Are you going to pick those up?"

"Yes, of course-" Felix replied, kneeling down to gather up the pens without further question. He neatly placed them on the counter, perfectly symmetrical.

"Well, everything seems to be in order. Are you sure there's nothing you need before I go? Perhaps a pen pot?"

"We're fine, thanks," Orion told him, flatly, trying to get him out of the room as quick as possible.

"Very well, don't be afraid to ask if you do."

"I won't be."

"Thank you for your time-"

"You're welcome."

And with that final line, the door was closed and locked behind him. Orion stayed by the door for a second or two, listening to Felix's shoes tip-tap on the floor until he got to the next room and began to recite the same lines once more. What a job.

It was only upon returning to his bedside that Orion fully processed the fact that Leo was not in the room. Where he would have gone at such an hour was a mystery, but since they resided on a heap of metal floating in outer space, he couldn't have gone far.

Orion sat down on his bed with a loud huff, running his hands over his face as the recollection of his dream that night flooded back to him.

There he was, at the end of the main concourse of the Exodus, gazing upon the destruction before him. The whole station was ablaze, flames creeping up the walls, reaching right up to the ceiling. He couldn't budge from that spot, feet stuck to the floor as if cemented there, no matter how hard he willed himself to move. And eventually, when the heat grew too intense, the huge window in the lounge blew out and Orion was sucked out into space, watching helplessly as the flaming space station became just another star in the sky. In his pyjamas, too. He was always in his pyjamas.

And somehow, floating alone in the void out there, Orion felt absurdly calm. That was when he woke up to the knock on the door.

With another sigh, he reached into his bedside table drawer and retrieved a small notepad in which he logged particularly vivid dreams. Flicking through the pages only revealed more similar ones. They usually happened under stress. Leo had encouraged him to start writing them down a while back, and to some extent it helped.

He started out with the simple sentence *'there was a big fire'* and then paused. No. No, 'big' didn't quite encapsulate it. He crossed it out and corrected himself with 'massive' written over the top. *'There was a massive fire on the Exodus. All my friends were trapped inside.'*

He thought for a while, bit the end of his pen and scribbled down *'Just like back home.'* before chucking the book back in the drawer.

Orion spent his younger years in a modest house, in Ruhigdorf, with his parents. His mother had been a great mathematician; Levi Goldschmidt met her in Seoul on his travels and invited her to move to the village when it was built, where she met Orion's father – a man with a passion for composing. Orion had lived in Ruhigdorf his entire life, but occasionally his family would take him out of town on a trip to the beach or to the city to watch a musical performance at some theatre or other. Although he was a little too young to really appreciate it at the time.

What he wouldn't give to be at an orchestral performance right now.

It was a cold, winter's night when it happened. There he stood, in the middle of the road, in his pyjamas, looking back at his childhood home burning away, the flames a stark contrast against the midnight sky.

And if he closed his eyes now, he could still see it.

He might have gone back inside to try and save his parents if a hand hadn't tugged him away before he had the chance.

To this day, he didn't know who it was that pulled him to safety, leading him all the way to Jonah's house with the rest of the surviving group, but if he found out who it was someday, he would have to remember to thank them for saving his life.

Slowly, Orion rose to his feet. In times such as these, it calmed him to re-read a note that he kept. From the rubble of his former home, he had salvaged his violin in its case, and tucked behind the instrument itself was a folded piece of paper. A

slightly tattered piece of paper, sure, but it was the
only thing Orion really had left.

"To our little virtuoso, Orion,
We know that music can be difficult sometimes, but
if you keep trying and never give up, we know that
you'll be a master violinist someday.
We're proud of you, son, and we'll always be right
behind you.
With love from mother and father."

Chapter 9

"Mason. *Mason!*"

Stopping in her tracks, Mason turned towards the source of the voice that had called her, half whisper, half shout.

"What?"

And there was Leo, hurrying towards her in a swift trot like an awkward horse, lifting his knees up high. Patiently, Mason waited for him to catch up.

"I changed my mind," he told her, gravely.

"Changed your... mind?"

The long concourse stretched behind him, all the way down to the lounge. The doors of the pub were opened, ready for the first customers of the day, and the few early birds walking around went about minding their own business. Despite being a relatively small group, the residents of the Exodus didn't do much in the way of socialisation.

Leo lowered his voice to avoid eavesdroppers, though they were far enough removed from anybody else to not be overheard.

"To speak to Jonah," he whispered, *"I want to come with you."*

"I see."

He drew his head back, suddenly becoming evidently concerned.

"You haven't been already, have you?"

But Mason shook her head.

"I was just about to."

"Good. Great, I mean. Shall we?"

She turned to the staircase and Leo followed gingerly after her.

Jonah's quarters were situated on the floor above the rest of the guests'. Since it was originally put there to be a family suite for the Goldschmidts, it boasted multiple rooms, which were now used only by Jonah.

The fourth floor also housed the rooms of the staff of the Exodus, though with the limited number of guests currently aboard, a lot of these were vacant. Mason should have been residing here, but upon learning about the move to the interstellar cruise liner, she had managed to convince Jonah to let her stay with Cass. She may have been a technician, but she was the family's guardian first and foremost.

There it was, at the end of the corridor, the grand door to the Goldschmidt quarters. With Felix out and about doing the room inspections, Jonah would have no choice but to come to the door himself. It could not have been timed better.

The camera intercom at the side of the door lit up as Mason and Leo approached. An addition by Jonah, evidently a camera fanatic.

Not giving it a glance, Mason briskly knocked on the contemporary panelled door and awaited a response.

"So, what should I say?" Leo asked, shifting his weight from foot to foot.

"You haven't thought of a script?"

"...No, I'm afraid not."

Mason gave him a look of disappointment as the lock of the door clicked open.

"Just let me do the talking."

Jonah Goldschmidt had the appearance of a man who had chopped down many trees in his lifetime and did not own a single razor blade. He squinted down at his android guests below thick, angry eyebrows, and frowned at them, tight-lipped.

"What do you want?" He asked, gruffly, scratching his bearded face.

"Leo and I just had some concerns."

"What kind of concerns?"

"Just about the supply delivery that usually arrives around this time. We noticed that it seems to be delayed and were wondering what might have caused-"

"You don't have any business worrying about that. Have those gossipers downstairs been planting rumours in your little mechanical head?"

"No, sir. Just a concern of mine. But I hear the eating places are beginning to run short on a few ingredients..."

"They'll just have to use what they have more wisely."

"We'd like answers," Leo put in, stepping forwards in a sudden, fleeting display of confidence.

Jonah's attention turned to him swiftly, eyes locking onto his.

"Listen, Leonardo-"

"It's Leopold actually."

"I don't care. Listen. I don't know what you're accusing me of but whatever it is, you're wrong." He jabbed one of his hairy fingers into Leo's chest. "I let you stay in my house and now I'm stuck on a space station with you. Both of you. The least you can do is not bother me with your misguided rumours. And don't start spreading any, either."

Leo took a step backwards, his catlike eyes darting back and forth between Jonah and Mason.

"I see," Mason said, flatly.

On that note, Jonah began to retreat back into his quarters, looking back over his shoulder to tell the two androids to go home before he closed the door behind him.

"Let's go, Leo."

"...Right. Coming."

The brevity of their exchange with Jonah had managed to reveal nothing about the Exodus' predicament, but a whole lot about the man's personality.

The two walked in silence, Leo softly rubbing the spot on his chest where he had been violently poked. And only when they were out of range of the intercom did he speak again.

"He was dodging the question."

"I noticed," Mason replied.

"So what do we do now?" Leo started, but she shushed him quietly as they descended the stairs, hearing Felix's voice. He was turned with his back to them, a little way along the mezzanine.

"Yes, sir. I'll keep an eye on them, sir."

"That's probably about us, I suspect."

"I think you're right, Leo."

With as little sound as possible, they made their way down the next flight of steps down to the second floor, and then to the first. Getting caught discussing the matter in front of Felix would be a dangerous mistake to make.

"We'll have to be careful where we talk about this," Mason told Leo when they stopped in the lobby. The Exodus was beginning to awaken at this point, most of its residents roused by their room inspections and now flocking downstairs for an early breakfast.

"You think there's really something going on, then?" Leo hummed.

"I think so. But like Jonah said. Don't go spreading rumours. We don't want mass panic," Mason warned him as she brushed herself down.

"Of course."

"This is where we part ways for the day."

"...We do?"

"I have to go to work."

"Ah," Leo smiled, awkwardly, "I forgot about that."

He took her gloved hand in both of his and very tenderly shook it.

"Thank you for letting me come with you. I apologise for not being much help," he told her.

"That's okay," Mason replied, blankly.

"Have a good day at work, won't you."

"I will certainly try."

And with that he released her hand and departed with a bow, as was his custom.

It was about that time in the morning where Cass would be getting ready for work. In fact, she'd be coming downstairs any minute now. If she saw Mason up and about on the main floor, she would get suspicious for sure. So as the time struck exactly seven, she stepped into the lift that would take her down to the sublevel. It was at this moment, too, that the morning announcement played over the speakers scattered about the Exodus.

"Good morning, residents of the Space Station Exodus," came Felix's voice, crackling through the tinny speaker inside the lift compartment, *"It is currently seven a.m. on the tenth of October, twenty-eighty-four. The weather for our friends back home is… mild. Have a good day and stay safe."*

'Stay safe', Mason repeated in her head. As if you could get yourself into serious trouble here, on a luxury space cruise. The most imminent danger was the threat of accidentally spilling a hot beverage on yourself.

The lift thumped to a halt as it reached the lower floor and its doors slowly slid open. The ceilings down here were lower, the floors and walls plain and sterile in contrast with the sleek modern décor upstairs. Not that it mattered. Nobody aside from the crew came down here. Apart from Cass sometimes.

Mason passed the doorway to the laundry room, hearing the thumping of the washing machines as she went by, until she reached the doorway to her workshop. The entrance to another day of sitting on her own.

<u>Chapter 10</u>

"Good work today."

"Thanks," Cass smiled as she untied her apron. With only 30 or so people on the Exodus, the café wasn't a particularly busy place to work. Still, being the only barista there, Cass had plenty of chance to prove herself as a hard worker.

"There'll be some alterations to the menu tomorrow," her manager, Mr Dupont, told her, looking over the top of his glasses.

"...What kind of alterations?"

"Just the removal of some items. Caramel latte, double chocolate mocha, affogato al caffe… desserts too."

"Why?"

"Ingredient shortages. We're cutting back. Not just us, the pub, too."

"...Is there anything else we're missing?"

"We have enough of the essentials to last a while. We just have to ration them."

"Ration?"

Dupont made his way over to the door where he unfolded a glossy sheet of paper and began to tape it up on the glass.

"What's that?" Cass asked, laying down her folded apron on the counter and moving closer.

"A notice for customers."

"About what?"

"Read it yourself."

Dupont stepped away from the door, opening it to let Cass out as he did.

"See you in the morning, Cass."

The door shut behind her, 'closed' sign knocking against the glass as it did, but she lingered a little longer to read the notice.

"Dear customers," the bold heading opened, *"Due to a shortage in ingredients, please limit yourself to one drink and one dessert per day. We apologise for any inconvenience this causes. Thank you."*

Something about the message sent a shiver up Cass' spine. Maybe because it was spelled out so clearly it struck home a little more directly. And the word her manager had used. Ration.

The only time Cass had heard of rationing before was in lessons about historical wars, back as a kid. She remembered being shown a photograph of a little ration book and thinking about how awful it must have been to only be allowed a set amount of food. The little boxes listing bread, meat, eggs, fats…

But it wouldn't get to that point. She knew that.

Heart weighing heavily in her chest, Cass heaved a sigh and turned away. With nothing else to do with her day, the only thing left to do was to go back to her room.

Nobody else was around, all probably having their evening meal. Orion and Leo would be practising for their seven o'clock performance so she couldn't even visit them.

She reached the door and heard it unlock when she approached, reacting to the key-card in her pocket without her even having to retrieve it.

Her side of the room was still cluttered with paint tubes and canvases, exactly how she had left it. The painting of the playground behind her house could, by all means, be called finished at this point. But Cass felt that there was still something missing from the composition.

With a huff, she sat down on the corner of the bed to stare at the picture, hoping that the finishing touch would occur to her if she looked for long enough. She only hoped she wouldn't have to start rationing her creativity to save on canvases too.

When the door to the room opened again it took her a minute to register it. Her eyes flicked to the LED clock on the wall and she found it to be considerably later than she had expected. A whole hour and she still hadn't come up with any ideas, completely preoccupied with wondering how she was going to break the news to Mason that she was right about the supply plane.

She muttered a lacklustre 'hey' as she heard Mason hang up her jacket.

"What are you doing?"

"Just thinking." Cass turned her head to look at Mason, who stood there straight-faced as usual, with a large book under her arm.

"I thought we could talk..." Mason began, evidently reluctant, but before she could continue, she was cut off.

"We should."

Taken aback by the words' bluntness, Mason stayed silent.

"At work today I got told we're running out of food. The whole *station's* running out of food. And now we're going to have to start rationing it."

"...Yes."

Cass' face shifted from worried to indignant.

"You knew?"

"It's due to the delay of the supply plane. That's all."

"What do you mean 'that's all'?"

"Leo and I have been... looking into it."

"And you didn't tell me?"

Mason paused. It had been a mistake to assume she could get away with keeping her little 'investigation' a secret from Cass forever.

"I didn't want to worry you."

"You thought I just wouldn't find out? I have a right to know what's going on."

"I-"

"You can't just... go around keeping secrets from me, I thought we were friends."

"We are."

Neither spoke for a minute. Mason slowly took the book from under her arm and set it down on the table.

"I- *we* think that Jonah might be… up to something."

"Jonah? Uncle Jonah?"

"Yes."

"Now you're just being ridiculous. I know uncle Jonah doesn't socialise with everyone else, but he's my uncle. What, you think he's trying to starve everyone?"

"I don't know."

"He's family, Mason. That's not what family does to each other."

"Cass..."

"He let us all stay in his house after the you-know-what happened, did you forget about that? He's not a bad guy. You make him out to be some sort of evil mastermind. He just keeps to himself because he lost dad. Get over it, Mason."

Mason slowly rubbed her hands together, struggling to find anything to say.

"Why are you so obsessed with playing detective?"

"I'm not… obsessed."

"All you care about is acting like you're Sherlock Holmes and walking around with your hands behind your back. You never stop to check in on your friends, ever. Maybe you don't know how to care, but some of us have feelings, you know? Just… stop it."

The room fell silent, the only audible sound the shuffling of the residents of the neighbouring room and the continuous dull whirr of Mason's circuitry.

"...Sorry."

"Yeah," Cass frowned, darting her eyes away to look at the canvas on her easel once more.

"Maybe I should… go."

"Yeah. I think you should."

*

On the main floor of the Exodus, between the mini arcade and the information desk, was a room filled to the brim with computers.

Rows of cubicles with ceiling-height dividing walls lined the right side of the premises, while the left was home to an automated check-in desk, some vending machines and an impressively long couch.

A cyber-café of sorts, the place was almost always completely barren. It was a place to retreat to when the confines of your designated cabin became too much to bear, and the lounge just wouldn't cut it. Yet it was so seldom used by anybody it felt more like a space-filler, something just placed there to liven up an otherwise empty shopfront. The concept of a cyber café had fallen out of style years ago, now only a retro pleasure.

But today, right in the corner of the room, one of the computers was active. In the darkened cubicle sat a slender figure, illuminated only by the light of the screen. His waistcoat was hung over the back of the chair and his neck bow was untied, hanging loose over his shoulders. As he stared across at the wide, curved monitor, the familiar and reassuring face of Dr Hatsumi gazed back at him with a fondness in his eye.

"Something is on your mind. Isn't it?" he hummed, voice crackling as he took a pondering breath. The doctor's age was beginning to creep up on him at last. Not that that would stop him running GASO as long as he could, he had never been one to give up and lie down. Even after he lost his leg years ago, he had simply built himself a new one.

Leo had to admire his determination. Even if the majority of his life on the planet had been spent being a carer and running errands, hardly spending more than an hour a week in the company of the scientist, he still held a lot of respect in his heart for the man.

"It's nothing," Leo told him.

Hatsumi did not seem convinced. He raised his teacup to his mouth and the android automatically mirrored the action.

"I'll give you a minute… to think about it."

Leo averted his gaze, letting it drift aimlessly about the cubicle, but ultimately finding nothing to focus on. Eventually he settled watching the tea in his paper cup swirl around gently when he tilted his hand.

"Hatsumi," he started, formally. Out of respect, he avoided using the doctor's given name, although Hatsumi had told him numerous times in the past he had full permission to do so, "...Can androids... love?"

A smile spread across Hatsumi's face and he leaned back in his chair, closing his eyes.

"Aren't you the best person to answer that question, Leo?"

"I don't know. I mean, it's not *me* I'm worried about."

"Ah. I see. Who is it?"

"Well. For instance... Mason. Just as an example."

"That's a difficult question, son. One I don't think I am capable of answering."

"Why?"

"I don't know every detail of every line of code Levi put into the AI. Mason is a lot different to you, just as humans differ from person to person."

"I know. I know, I just thought it would be... simpler than that."

Through all the time he'd known Mason, he'd never once heard her express affection to anyone, or even be remotely emotionally affected by anything. Even the fire, which took the life of her creator, seemed to only sit in her mind as a historical event, rather than the tragedy it was.

"If you want an answer to your question, Leo. You'll have to find it yourself."

"How?"

"You'll figure it out. Try not to think about it too logically."

Leo cracked a smile.

"Interesting advice coming from a scientist."

"I'm only human."

The timer pop-up on the monitor signalled that the computer would remain active for only three minutes longer. These once-in-a-blue-moon video calls with Hatsumi always flew by too fast.

"Just one more thing before I go," Leo gingerly started. He'd been pondering bringing up the subject for the whole call, but who knew when their schedules would allow them the pleasure of speaking again?

"Go on."

"About the supply plane. Why hasn't it docked yet? Is there a hold-up?"

"The supply-? Why, we were told it wasn't needed."

"What?"

"We never sent it up. We were told explicitly that the Exodus had more than enough provisions and to hold off until it was necessary."

"Who told you that?"

"Well, Jonah, of course."

"...He told you that?"

"Yes."

Leo slowly set down his almost-empty cup, eyes unfocused and unblinking.

"Leo? What's wrong?"

But before he could even begin to explain, he heard the sound of the door opening with a chime, followed by the soft footsteps of somebody approaching the cubicles.

Leo thought back to what he'd overheard Felix say that morning. How he would 'keep an eye on them'. Quite literally, in his case.

"Anyway… I should be going," he said instead, as casually as he could, "Send me a message when you're free to do this again, alright?"

"It may not be for a while, Leo. I have a *very* busy month ahead of me, you know."

"Of course you do," the android smiled, a cheap attempt to mask his worry, "See you sometime, Hatsumi."

"Take care of yourself, Leo."

"I will."

And with that, the call was ended, headphones hung up and the computer powered down. Composing himself, Leo got to his feet, took his waistcoat from the back of the chair and swiftly put it back on. He could still hear the shuffling of feet outside and dreaded opening the door and walking out with Felix's stare drilling into him as he went. But he pulled himself together and stepped out of the cubicle, grasping the paper cup for safety like an anchor.

"Leo. Just in time."

"Orion?"

"Who else? I came to fetch you so we wouldn't be late for our show," Orion said, leaning back the door of the empty cubicle opposite Leo, "I worried for a moment you might have been spending so much time with Mason you started to pick up her terrible timekeeping."

Leo scoffed, shaking his head as he trailed after his friend.

"How was the catch-up session?" Orion asked, holding the main door open for him.

"...Good," Leo nodded. He didn't need to worry Orion about what Hatsumi had told him. Not now. Not before a show. Later, then he'd tell him, "Yeah. It was good."

Chapter 11

The Exodus pub rang with the melody of violin; a slow, gentle tune for the evening. Orion played his instrument like an extension of himself, every move natural and seemingly effortless.

Leo stood beside him, softly singing the words to Patrick Watson's *Je Te Laisserai Des Mots* as his hand gently cradled the old-fashioned microphone in front of him. His eyes sleepily scanned over the room, taking note of every face that observed him back. The place was almost full tonight, near every table occupied. Just to the right he could see the waitress taking somebody's order, and to the left a young woman with glasses trying to enjoy a slice of toast with pate whilst the ever-chatty Tomas gossiped beside her.

Leo spied the door open from the corner of his eye and he watched as Mason entered, earlier than usual. She didn't look back at him, but she took her usual seat at the table facing the stage. Even when she was seated, she hardly looked his way.

Not letting it phase him, Leo went on with the song. It wasn't like Mason to ignore him when she came into the pub. He wondered if he'd done something wrong.

The song drew to a close and Orion started up the next one. It would be an arduous wait through the set list before Leo could greet his friend. He kept his eyes trained on her for the most part, making sure she stayed. And never once did she look his way.

The applause of the pub's patrons bid farewell to another night's performance as Leo and Orion stepped back through the velvet curtains to the dark little backstage room, scarcely more than an alcove. While Orion methodically tucked his violin back in its case and gathered everything up carefully, Leo had already departed. He drifted past the tables like a wisp of smoke, eventually coming to Mason's table and pulling up a chair.

"So," he started, brushing himself down, "Where's Cass?"

"We… aren't speaking," Mason replied, quietly. She sat with her elbows on the table, chin resting on clasped hands.

Leo tilted his head to the side and leaned in a little closer,

"Why, what happened?"

Mason's good eye finally rolled upwards to look at him.

"Just. Nothing. Just a disagreement." She sat up straight, putting on that facade like the matter wasn't important. She knew Leo could see straight through it, "Well, our investigation isn't a secret any more. She's a little… put out… that we didn't tell her."

"You were only trying to avoid worrying her," Leo reasoned.

"Yeah, but she's right. First she loses her mother, then her father and her home, the last thing she needs is me keeping secrets from her. That's not the only thing, either. She's not happy we're investigating Jonah specifically."

"I didn't think they were friends."

"They're not. They're family."

Mason gave a low noise of lamentation, shifting her weight and choosing to look at the wall on her right instead of her companion. She absently fiddled with one of the staples that held her face together.

"I've been thoughtless," she said, "Cass is right. I just don't care enough, that's the problem."

Leo was about to tell her that that wasn't true, but he stopped himself for fear of lying. He didn't know whether the statement was true or false at all.

"Maybe we've been looking in the wrong place. Maybe Jonah has nothing to do with it after all, maybe it's all under control," Mason said, running her hands over her face, "I don't know..."

"We were looking in the right place," Leo told her, sternly, and she parted her fingers slightly so that she could look across at him.

"What do you mean?"

"I spoke to Dr Hatsumi. I asked him about the supply plane. He said they never sent it up; you know who told them not to?"

"Who?"

Leo leaned in close and lowered his voice.

"Our pal Jonah. Apparently… *he* told GASO that we have enough without it up here. And we all know that's not true..."

Mason's eye widened.

"You told him it was a mistake, though, right? You told him about the situation?"

"I… couldn't. I didn't know if Felix was listening in, I- I'm sorry."

"It's okay. It just means that you're going to have to get back in touch with GASO and tell them. Easy."

"You say 'me' like you're not going to help me."

"I can't, Leo. Not any more."

"Because of Cass?"

"Yes."

"But… I..."

"You just have to make a call, that's all."

"What if they don't believe me?"

"They will. Trust me."

Leo sat back and finally nodded resolutely. If making a simple call was what it took to save the Exodus from starvation, he would just have to do it. Over Mason's shoulder, he could see Orion talking with the Exodus' oldest resident. At least, he was being talked *at*. Awkwardly, he managed to excuse himself from the conversation and began to make his way over to the table.

"I should get going," Mason said as she rose from her seat, chair legs scraping across the wooden floor.

"You won't stay to talk for a while?"

"No, I… think I'd better leave. Sort out some stuff..." She shot a glance back over her shoulder before looking back to Leo, "You should be honest with Orion, too." And with those last words, she left.

Outside the pub, a four-armed figure stood by the window.

The lens of Felix's eye contracted as he zoomed out his vision from where he had been observing an interesting conversation. Content with what he'd seen, he silently turned on his heels and left before anybody even realised he'd been there.

Chapter 12

Cass lay on top of her bedsheets, staring up at the spotlights on the ceiling. She'd been here a while now. She didn't know what she was expecting to happen, whether she thought Mason would walk back through the door and apologise or whether Orion would knock and ask what was wrong. But no. Lying and staring at the ceiling had accomplished nothing.

Groggily, she sat up straight, momentarily losing vision from the movement. She didn't know how long she'd been waiting on nothing, but it had been over an hour for certain. The room was getting dark and the canvas on the easel was still missing that last addition.

From the corner of her vision, Cass eyed the large book that Mason had left on the table. She hadn't seen it before – she would remember a book like that – and curiosity was getting the better of her, so she got to her feet and dragged herself over.

The book was leather bound, tied closed in a knot. And on the front were embossed the words 'The Goldschmidt Family'.

Tentatively, Cass lifted the cover, and a piece of interleaving paper fluttered as it opened. Peeling back the delicate sheet revealed a large glossy photograph.

The house.

Its doorway took centre stage, ivy creeping up the walls, and about the building the trees curled around. The last time Cass had seen this house, the windows had been black, the roof caved in and the insides completely gutted. She hardly remembered what it had looked like before…

Slowly, with eyes still glued to the book, Cass made her way back to her bed. She flicked on the lamp on her bedside table and slipped her legs under the covers.

Flicking over a few pages, she landed on a collection of baby photos. A birth announcement card was taped to the left page, with the details of newborn Cassiopeia Goldschmidt. Across the page were various other pictures that any new parent would capture. Baby with mum, baby with dad, baby shoving a silver rattle in her mouth, baby's first time trying yoghurt. But one stood out to her amongst the others.

Mason, sat in the old rocking chair in the nursery, little Cass cradled in her arms, the morning light illuminating them both. Her mouth didn't smile, but that wasn't uncommon for her. Instead, she looked almost fascinated by the tiny life entrusted to her, mixed with some resolute stare.

That look.

Cass had seen it a lot recently. Since things around the ship started getting all weird. The last time she'd acted like this – whatever *this* was – had been back in Jonah's house all those years ago.

Cass wondered why she'd never seen this book before. Just another thing Mason was keeping from her. Plenty more where that came from, she could only imagine.

With a sigh, she turned a couple of pages. There was a large time gap between one page and the next, where the photos containing her mother abruptly stopped appearing. She didn't remember much of her mother, for better or for worse, and what she could remember was foggy and obscured. She wondered, sometimes, what life on the Exodus would be like if she was still here. Would she know what to do about the crisis? Would she have told Cass about everything?

Levi dealt with the loss of Samantha by working his fingers to the bone and Cass didn't see much of him most days, save for the rare occasions they would go on a day trip out somewhere, so most of her time was spent in android company.

Cass noted one photo in a familiar setting. The playground behind the house. The very same she'd painted earlier that day. She could see herself, not older than six or seven, sat at the top of the slide, while Mason crouched at the bottom, ready to catch her. The day she faced her fear of the slide...

Carefully, Cass removed the photo from the corner tabs to take a closer look. There was something almost ethereal about it. The slight fog in the air, the trees reaching up far past what fit in frame. And there was Mason, in a long black coat, not quite smiling. It never quite came naturally to her.

She never really knew when to smile, not back then. She never knew how to play with Cass, not how Sam did. And she was never soft or warm. But she was always there, doing the best she knew how to.

Cass placed the picture back in the album and leaned back against the wall with a deep breath. Maybe what she'd said *had* been a little harsh. Even if her point still stood. Mason would be home soon and then they would have to talk about it. But until then, she still had an album to look through.

She pulled the covers up and over her shoulders and rolled over onto her side to leaf through the rest of the pages by warm lamplight.

It wasn't long before she'd fallen asleep with the book still grasped firmly in her hands.

Chapter 13

Making a call. That was all. Easy. Leo had done much scarier things than that in his life. Even just recently, he'd stood face-to-face with Jonah Goldschmidt. He'd even escaped a burning village. Why should this be any different?

He'd decided to leave it until the morning. It was getting late by the time he'd finished explaining the predicament to Orion, and he didn't want to wake anyone at GASO with his distress signal. He left the room when Orion was still sleeping, equipped with a short script he'd scribbled down on a piece of paper to remind him what to say.

He took a seat in one of the booths in the cyber-café (once again empty aside from him) and straightened his turtle-neck. He had GASO's contact for emergencies, as did Mason, Cass and Felix, but he'd never used it before. He didn't even know anyone who worked there except Hatsumi. Leo hoped that he would be the one to pick up the call, but he knew it was unlikely.

With a decisive nod, he opened up the VoIP software for making calls back to Earth. But when the homepage greeted him, he also noted a large red banner at the top of the screen informing him that the computer had no connection to the Internet.

Strange, he thought, as the connection in the Exodus hadn't failed him for the entire time he'd lived here. But no matter. Thinking nothing of it, he simply opened up the settings to reconnect. But not even the name of the network appeared for him to select.

Perhaps a fault with the machine itself.

Although it was a slight inconvenience, Leo switched to the computer in the neighbouring stall. But that one gave him the same results, as did the next.

With all options exhausted, he gathered himself together and left the cyber-café, stepping out onto the main floor of the Exodus. Across from him, Felix stood in front of a large notice board, pinning up a poster of some sort.

"Felix!"

He turned around, large purple eye wide and unblinking, like he'd been caught red-handed.

"Ah- Leo. If this is about the food predicament, there's nothing I can do..."

"It's not," Leo replied, "For once. Is there a problem with our Internet connection? Did the password change or something? I can't connect, I was just trying to make a call to… a friend."

Felix's eye flicked to the side as if he was listening to something before he looked back up to Leo, straight faced.

"I'll look into it."

"When do you think it'll be fixed?"

"I said I'll look into it."

Somewhat astounded by Felix's sharp response, Leo took a step back.

"Of course," he nodded, "Thanks."

Felix had a lot on his plate, he knew. This problem was probably adding to a whole mountain of others. He left then, leaving Leo alone facing the notice board.

The poster he'd pinned up caught Leo's eye.

'Please remember to ration!' was written in big bold font, and then underneath, *'Don't take more than is strictly necessary for you and your room-mates. We are currently experiencing a shortage of provisions, but we are working on this issue. We apologise for any inconvenience.'*

'Working on it'. Leo scoffed. The news wasn't exactly surprising in itself, but it somewhat impressed him that Jonah was actually publicly acknowledging the problem. He'd have thought the man would do anything to save face. Not that Jonah had much to lose, what with the rumours going around, all sparked by Tomas. Astounding how they circulated despite Tom being a known scandalmonger. His theory spread, for lack of a better term, like wildfire. In fact, just beside the poster was a hand-written note proclaiming *'Jonah Goldschmidt is a stone-cold killer!'*.

The other residents of the Exodus could say all they liked, but at the end of the day none of them had the nerve to look Jonah in the eye, never mind stand up to him.

Leo knew that the responsibility of getting to the bottom of whatever was going on fell on his shoulders. Mason had trusted him with that. And he'd be torn asunder before he let her down.

*

Felix stepped cautiously into the office of the Exodus' commander. All eight of his computer monitors splashed bright blue light around the room, every screen angled in to face Jonah. One of them streamed Felix's vision, and, as he looked right into it, it created a sort of infinite loop that was oddly mesmerising.

Felix didn't need to announce his presence. Jonah knew he was there already, and had watched him approach the door. He didn't even turn around to speak to him.

"Why are you here, Felix?"

"I thought it would be the safest place to speak to you, sir. Mason has remained uninvolved in the situation since yesterday. Leo is still a problem. I believe he has been trying to contact GASO…"

"I am aware, I was listening."

"Sorry, sir. As you know, the… uh… rumours about you… have continued to circulate. In fact, I'd say they have even begun to gain traction. Don't you think that cutting off communications might raise suspicion..?"

"It won't be a problem."

Felix's eye fluttered around the room and he began to rub his hands, as was his habit when disconcerted. The tall shelves and the many monitors seemed to stare down at him in the way a group of seagulls might crowd around a slice of unattended bread.

"Are you sure this is what you want to do, sir?"

Jonah tensed in his large office chair. He took his hands off his keyboard for once to clench and unclench his fists in bitter annoyance.

"Don't antagonise me, Felix. Did you run the checks like I told you?"

"Yes, sir. Everything's in order. When will we..?"

"Soon. I want you to pack for three days and change the codes for all the other pods. Do you understand?"

"Of course, sir."

Felix turned to leave, but was stopped before he could reach the door.

"And Felix…"

"Yes, sir?"

"I'll be watching."

<u>Chapter 14</u>

Mason withdrew to her room at mid-day to wait out her lunch break, recognising that her usual time out at the pub with Cass probably wasn't on the cards today. Cass herself was most likely spending the time either watching Leo and Orion or putting her feet up in the lounge, enjoying some way overdue time to herself.

But when Mason stepped through the door, Cass' shoes were already placed on the mat.

"Hi Mason."

"Cass. You're home."

She sat perched on the edge of her bed, reading a comic, lunch half-eaten beside her, calmer than Mason had expected.

"Cass, I'm sorry," Mason told her, clasping her hands behind her back. She'd had enough time over that morning and the night before to formulate what she wanted to say, she only hoped it would be right.

"I am too."

Mason paused.

"What I said was too harsh, we should have talked about it together, I'm sorry," Cass continued, laying her book down.

"You were right, though. I've always prioritised dealing with the situation over checking in on you, and I shouldn't have." Mason paused to remember the words she'd carefully planned, "I'll do better in the future."

Cass softly smiled, putting her feet up on the edge of the bed and resting her chin on her knees. And if Mason could have breathed a sigh of relief, she would have.

"Thanks, Mason. I appreciate it."

"I've been thinking about what you said before. About being able to care… and I thought about back when you were small, after your mother died, and I used to take you to the playground behind the house. That time you fell off the swing and scraped your knees, I was worried. I wasn't worried because of what Levi might say, I was worried because I cared about you. And I haven't stopped caring. I hope you know that."

"I know. I've always known that, I think."

"I know I'm not your mother, Cass-" she started, but she was cut off.

"But you don't have to be."

Mason smiled, just how she'd prepared herself to do when finally relieved from the fetters of guilt.

"So we're good?"

"Yeah, we're good... Thank you, by the way."

"For what?"

"Trying to keep an eye on me," Cass grinned.

"I do my best."

Mason pried her boots off using her heels and stepped over to the kitchenette, fetching a mug from the cupboard and a packet of malt drink powder. While it didn't entail her favourite hobby of holding a tiny espresso cup, it was good to have something larger that she could sit down and enjoy at the same time as Cass ate. It was the closest they could get to having dinner together.

"I've dropped the whole investigation thing, by the way," Mason told her as the water boiled, "Leo's taking care of it."

Cass' face creased with concern.

"Will he be okay on his own?" she asked.

"He's perfectly capable, Cass." Mason looked over her shoulder to give a reassuring smile, "He'll manage just fine."

And on the easel, the painting of the playground had finally been completed with the addition of two figures.

*

The Exodus lounge was simmering with life as the people who took their luncheon outside the eating establishments softly chattered amongst themselves. Above the elevator in the lobby, the large clock displayed the time as two minutes past one, wrapping up lunch.

After his and Orion's regularly scheduled performance at the pub, Leo hadn't stuck around to converse with the patrons as he usually did. Instead, he slipped out of the door and stationed himself by the entrance to the lounge, facing into it.

From his back pocket, he pulled out his phone and flipped the camera to the front, angling it just right so that he could look behind him right down to the lobby at the other end of the concourse. He kept one sharp eye trained on the screen, watching, waiting.

Uneasily, Leo fiddled with the neck of his polo-neck jumper, pulling the fabric away and then letting it fall back, almost rhythmically. The one lock of hair longer than the rest flopped down awkwardly over his left eye.

It took a while before he saw it. That short, stocky figure in plum suit, heading down the stairs with that trademark rapid, short-stepping gait. *'Like a pigeon'*, Orion always said.

Felix entered the lift to descend downstairs as Leo put his phone away and turned to follow him. After the severing of communication to the outside world that morning, Leo had been keeping an eye on Felix's movements. He seemed to be even more agitated than usual, which until now Leo hadn't thought possible.

When the lift came back up, he entered and the doors slid closed behind him. He didn't go down to the basement often, only the times when his voice required mending (usually after trying to hit the high notes in *Runaway* by Del Shannon), and Mason would have to fiddle around with it while Orion sat and watched from the corner with an exasperated look on his face.

To Leo's relief, when the doors opened again, they hardly made a sound. Felix was stood at the end of the dull, uninspired hallway, unlocking a door with his key card. From the sign above, Leo could gather it was the way to the escape pods. He'd never seen them in person before, but upon boarding the Exodus for the first time, he had been assured there was an extremely slim chance that they'd ever need to be used.

He craned his neck around the door frame, after Felix neglected to close the door properly, and peered inside.

The sheer size of the place explained why the rest of the basement was so small and cramped. Along the back wall were around eighteen bullet-shaped pods with steps leading up to them. The rounded front halves were poking outside of the wall, facing out into space, ready to be dispatched in case of an emergency. Each looked around the size to snugly fit 6 people. Adequate room for an escape pod, but even so, Leo wouldn't like to be stuffed in there with someone he didn't get along with.

Felix climbed the steps to each and addressed the interface beside every door, jabbing buttons and pressing numbers.

Maybe it was just routine maintenance, Leo thought to himself, and a wave of dread washed over him as he came to the realisation he probably shouldn't be down here. Shooting a glance back to the lift, he noted the CCTV camera above the doors slowly swivel left to right. What if Jonah was watching him right now? Then he'd be in major trouble.

Now all at once distressed and paranoid, he slipped behind the pilaster on the wall beside him, just out of view. All being well, Jonah will have been watching through Felix's view instead.

"That's the last one, sir," he heard Felix's voice come from the pod room, "Save yours, of course."

Hearing Jonah's responses would have provided some much-needed context, but that was a luxury Leo didn't have. From Felix's half of the conversation, he couldn't piece together the topic, especially with most audible words being 'of course' or 'yes, sir', but from the tone, he got the feeling it wasn't just routine inspection.

"The day after tomorrow? So soon? You're sure?" Felix somehow managed to sound even more wobbly than usual. He waited what felt like a century, listening to the response, before he finally spoke again, "Yes, I know, but… No. No doubts, sir, I assure you… I understand."

And that was the last thing he said before he stepped out of the room. As he turned to ensure the door was locked behind him, Leo became increasingly aware of the small distance between them, only the pilaster separating them. If he made the slightest sound, he would surely be heard. If he'd had the function of lungs, he would have held his breath.

It wasn't until he heard Felix's quick little footsteps hurry away that he cupped his hands over his nose and mouth and afforded himself the luxury of relaxing.

Chapter 15

The twelfth of October.

Nine-thirty in the morning.

Orion had told himself he wouldn't do anything careless.

But still, standing at the top of the stairs, leaning on one of the white marble columns, he could feel his resolve weaken. A thudding feeling in his chest, a rising heat in his head, the tension he was subconsciously holding in his jaw – all of it told him he wouldn't be able to hold this relative measure of composure for very long.

'Getting some fresh air' on the Exodus was, unsurprisingly, a touch difficult. No matter how much the air was circulated around the station, it was still just the same recycled stuff they'd been breathing for the past four years. The stuffy feeling in the atmosphere with no wind to blow it about never really went away. But even so, after his conversation with Leo that morning, Orion couldn't bear to sit in that poky cabin any longer.

Leo had told him all about what he'd seen and heard the day prior. About how Felix approached every escape pod but the last, about how perturbed he'd looked, and what he'd said about 'the day after tomorrow'. If that was true, then, well, today was the last day they had to do anything about it.

According to Leo, communications were still down, so contacting GASO for emergency assistance was still off the cards. And even so, it would take a good forty-eight hours for any craft to reach them from Earth, and by that time it might very well be too late.

The matter of the dwindling food supplies (now down to the last few dregs) was overshadowed, in Orion's mind, by the more immediate threat of whatever was happening tomorrow.

Not that he was that hungry anyway.

"Do we tell everyone else on board?" he'd asked, but in response Leo only shrugged his shoulders.

"I don't want to create a mass hysteria," he'd said.

'Don't they deserve to know?' Orion thought, *'Maybe they could help'*. But still, somewhere in the back of his mind, a little voice told him that, even after everything, maybe there wasn't anything wrong after all. What if they created a huge uproar over nothing? Then they'd be in all sorts of trouble. Inducing panic, spreading rumours against the captain… they'd never be able to look any of their neighbours in the eyes ever again. That was when he had excused himself.

Orion crossed his arms, pressing his chin to his chest and puffing out a loud sigh. The last thing he wanted to do was approach each and every resident of the Exodus one by one and tell them that they might all die tomorrow, but how would he feel in his heart if he didn't?

That was when that all-too-familiar figure passed him by.

The sight of Felix didn't make Orion's heart jump with joy at the best of times, but seeing him now was just kicking him when he was down.

The android was heading down from Jonah's room, clearly, to the main floor below, but as he prepared to descend the last staircase, a force stopped him.

Without thinking for a second, Orion found he had shot out his hand to seize the back of Felix's jacket collar. And without stopping to reconsider, he'd pulled him back to grab him by the shoulders.

Felix stared up at him with his one huge eye quivering, the six-inch height difference between them suddenly exceedingly evident.

"Hello," was all he managed to say after a couple of seconds of painful silence.

"What are the codes for the escape pods?" Orion snapped back, "I know you were messing around with those things, what were you doing?"

"That's- That's strictly on a need-to-know basis, Mr Sauer," Felix replied, with a look on his face like he'd just been told the date of his death.

"Well I need to know, camera boy."

"If you're concerned about something, I'm sure I can help."

"I'm concerned about why you've been messing around so much on this piece of space junk. First the missing supplies, then the coms cut-off, now this," Orion retorted, tilting his head and looking straight into the centre of the lens of Felix's eye, "I know you're listening, Jonah, and I want to know those codes."

"Can I go, please?" Felix quivered, "Please can you let me go?"

He shakily raised his back two arms in what looked like a surrender, but then slowly balled his hands into fists. First, he raised three fingers, then five, then two, then six...

Orion's face softened slightly, the glare in his eye vanishing. He watched as Felix kept flashing numbers at him, white gloved fingers flicking up and down. And eventually, after 12 numbers, he put his arms down by his sides.

"...How am I supposed to remember all that?" Orion asked. But Felix's eye widened in dread as he spoke.

"I'm sorry I can't help you… Orion," was his only response as he clasped his hands together over his chest. Jonah's voice in his earpiece was so loud that Orion could hear it, muffled, as the sound leaked out.

He dropped his hands from Felix's shoulders, defeated.

"It's OK, Felix. Sorry for the bother."

"Orion?"

Sharply, he turned around to see Cass standing a way down the hallway, grasping the strap of the bag slung over her shoulder.

As Orion turned away, Felix took a tentative step back, and when he realised it was safe to move, he hurriedly went on his way downstairs.

"What was *that* all about?" Cass asked.

"I don't… know." Orion ran his hands over his face and hung his head. He'd never known himself to act like that before, not even after his parents died. He'd never been confrontational in the slightest. But before he could continue to wallow in his guilt and self-pity, he felt a hand land on his arm.

"Should we go downstairs, get a coffee and talk about it?" Cass suggested, "You look like garbage."

"I haven't slept in days. And there isn't any coffee," Orion replied, dropping his hands to look up at her.

"Just water, then. Come on, it's the weekend, it's not like we have anything better to do."

Reluctantly, Orion agreed. From what Leo had told him, he wasn't to say anything to Cass about the issue. He wasn't sure how he was going to navigate a whole conversation without bringing up what was making his head feel like static.

To his relief, when they got down to the concourse, Felix was already out of sight. And when they entered the pub, it was completely barren apart from the bartender and one server in the corner scribbling in a notepad.

Cass insisted that having a straw with his water would make Orion feel better, so now he sat at one of the sticky tables he often looked at from onstage, head bowed, awkwardly sipping his drink. In the background, the speakers on the wall droned out some old, slow instrumental music that was probably supposed to be relaxing, but under the circumstances, just made Orion more aware of the life draining from his body as he sat there.

"What's this song, Orion?" Cass asked eventually in an attempt to break the ice. In her hand, she idly slid the lime slice around the rim of her glass until it wore away too much and fell to the table with a pathetic splat.

"I believe it's *Room With a View* by Russ Morgan."

"Can you play it?"

"I haven't tried."

"Maybe you should. You can probably find the sheet music online somewhere."

Orion leaned back in his chair, wrapping his arms around himself. He wasn't exactly sure whether there'd be time to learn a new song. He wasn't sure whether he'd ever play again.

"You're acting weird still," Cass said, flatly, in the sort of tone Mason had when she was trying to figure out if what she was about to say could be construed as rude or not, "Really, Orion. What's up? If this is about the whole 'my uncle is an arsonist' thing, you don't have to pretend it's not."

"You know about that?"

"Mason told me a couple of days ago. Did something come of it?"

"Yesterday, Leo said he followed Felix down to the basement and he was messing around with the escape pods down there. Changing the access codes or something," Orion eventually told her, deciding it was worth the risk of sharing, "Then he said something about 'the day after tomorrow'. Something's happening tomorrow, Cass, and I don't know what it is or how to stop it."

Cass' forehead lined with concern. Absent-minded, she reached up a hand to fidget with the cuffs on her ears.

"What do you think it could be? It could be nothing, right?"

"Or it could be something massive."

"Like what, though?"

"Like… like what if Jonah gets in his escape pod and leaves us all to starve up here?"

"Can't we call GASO and get them to come up?"

"All the coms are down, Leo hasn't been able to get a signal on the VoIP for days now. We keep trying. Whatever happens, it's down to us."

Cass fell silent. The song playing drew to a close. She knew Orion was right – anything could happen. The first course of action, she thought to herself, was to find out what it was. Which is exactly what Leo and Mason had been trying to do all this time. But with one day left, it was due time to kick into full gear.

"I think you should go and talk to anyone you find and see what they know, if anything," Cass said, "Maybe someone overheard Felix talking to Jonah or something. Just try and find out anything you can without causing a huge stir. I'll talk to Mason about the coms, she might be able to pull some hacker stunt and get us back online."

Orion nodded. It wasn't much of a plan, but it was pretty much the only option they had.

"Just. Don't start giving up, yeah?" Cass warned him, "'Cause I don't want to be stuck up here until I die. I wanna go back home someday. I wanna visit an art gallery and ride a horse and go… strawberry picking, or whatever it is we used to do for fun."

"Yeah…That sounds good." And though his voice was watery, Orion cracked a smile.

Chapter 16

"There's nothing I can do, Cass, I'm sorry."

"Nothing? Seriously? I thought you did, like… robot stuff."

"I do re-wiring and soldering, I'm no programmer. I put the pieces in the computers, I don't know how they work." Mason shrugged her shoulders and pulled an attempt at a sympathetic face, "I'm afraid I wasn't really made for that sort of job. If you need a coder, Hatsumi is who you have to talk to, but obviously that's not an option right now."

Cass released a heavy sigh, wringing her hands in agitation. Getting communication to Earth re-established would, at the very least, allow them to inform GASO what was going on. And if Jonah knew that GASO knew what he was doing, maybe he'd reconsider starving out the whole station. But as things were looking, there didn't seem to be much chance of cracking into the network at all.

"Is there anyone else on board who might be able to do it?" Cass enquired.

"Not unless someone's hiding some secret tech know-how, I wouldn't think so. Most of the people who have programming knowledge are still back on Earth with GASO."

It was true that, while the Goldschmidt Aeronautics and Space Organisation had lost the majority of its members in the fire, those who remained either lived in places near Ruhigdorf, or simply worked remotely, and hadn't had a reason to move onto the Exodus. Most of its current occupants were individuals and families who helped plan the village itself, cooks, architects and the children of Levi's friends, who had lost their parents and since grown up.

"We're pretty hopeless, aren't we, Mason? I mean, a barista, an android technician, a singer and a violinist trying to solve a mystery. We're like some sort of wacky sitcom cast..." Cass muttered, but when she gazed back at her friend, her head was tilted down towards her shoulder in one of her episodic inadvertent shut-downs.

It was anyone's guess how long she'd be out, so with a huff, Cass flopped down onto the couch beside her.

"Nice going, Mason," she groaned with a palpable tone of dismay. Usually in moments like these, Cass would retreat to her easel to create yet another painting, but today it would come as a surprise to no-one that she wasn't really in the mood for it.

*

Orion's quest to uncover new information had ended up a fruitless endeavour.

Due to the fact that Jonah mainly stayed cooped up upstairs, nobody had seen him around or heard anything from him. The only person who ever heard Jonah's voice was Felix.

It seemed nobody had overheard anything from *him,* either.

The sense of crisis Orion felt among his friends was not especially present in the rest of the Exodus' occupants, who were mainly just irate concerning the lack of food and other essentials. Nothing more and nothing less.

Despite the gnawing in the pit of his stomach, Orion refrained from telling anybody about the potential disaster that tomorrow could bring.

The only information he'd managed to glean was from the resident doctor, Dr Griffin, who had seen Felix in the lift taking large plastic crates full to the brim with supplies down to the basement. Orion thanked him for his help, but in reality, it provided little insight.

He had retreated to his room a little downtrodden, hoping that Cass was doing better than he was. He found himself drawn to the comfort of his violin, and though his hands shook and the notes came out wobbly, it helped his heart stop fluttering briefly. He soldiered through the evening show, but neither he nor Leo stuck around afterward.

And now here he was, curled up on the sofa, idly keeping his hands busy with the buttons on his sleeve cuffs while his mind wandered elsewhere. Usually after an evening show, he and Leo would play a game of chess.

But not tonight.

Leo himself had just finished drying the dishes and putting them away in silence. He neatly folded the tea towel and set it down on the counter. He seemed, in a way, somewhat disappointed that there were no more dishes left, and that he would now be forced to confront the awkward reality of the situation.

"Leo," Orion started, looking up at his friend from where he lay on the sofa, "Could you tell me a story?"

Leo looked over his shoulder, glasses catching the glare of the bright floor lamp in the corner.

"A story?..I suppose so."

He tucked the stray hair behind his ear and pulled up a chair. The legs knocked against the floor as he dragged it over and sat himself down to face Orion, hands clasped in his lap.

"Let's think… what's an interesting story…"

"No, no," Orion cut him off, "I want you to make one up."

"Make one up?" Leo's eyed widened slightly at the mere thought, "I suppose I could give it a try. Alright, here we go… well… once upon a time, there lived four harvest mice who were all best friends. They lived in a field and ate things like berries and whatever else mice eat. But then one winter it started to rain so heavily they knew it wouldn't be long until the field flooded.

The rain poured down and the mice were starting to get scared because there wasn't any place to take shelter. The closest safe space was a bridge just a mile away that they could see over on the horizon if they climbed up the stalks of wheat, but there was no chance of them walking there on time."

Orion couldn't help but crack a smile. There was something about the way Leo told tales, like a children's storyteller on TV, calmly and slowly in that whimsical syrupy voice, with neither too much nor too little enthusiasm. Being reluctantly drawn in was a given.

"Then what happened?"

"Well," Leo continued, "Fortunately the mice were very good builders. They all worked together as a team and made a raft out of grasses that would support all four of them, and a sail out of a leaf. And when the flood came, they all floated away."

"...And?"

"And they lived happily ever after, of course."

"Very sappy, Leo," Orion said, with the vaguest hint of a smirk, "And what would have happened to the mice had they not been good builders?"

"Well then they'd just have to learn to swim, I suppose."

"I don't know if we have time to learn how to swim, Leo," Orion breathed, and he let his eyes drift closed, leaving his friend on the chair to watch over him.

"No, Orion. I don't suppose we do."

Chapter 17

Thirteenth of October.

Seven a.m.

Leo had risen early that morning finding that the impending sense of dread that had been weighing on him for the past week had risen to new heights. While Orion still slept, he dressed, made himself an Americano – which he drained all in one go – and paced a few circles around the coffee table.

At eight a.m., when Orion had awoken, Leo departed their room with one goal dead set in his mind.

He stood in front of his neighbour's door, on the otherwise completely silent mezzanine. The only sound he could hear was the muffled shuffling of the pub being set up for the day downstairs.

Right now, there was nothing Leo wanted more than to be able to have a normal day. The actions that had seemed so mundane to him mere days ago he now longed for like a safety blanket. But he knew that today there would be no joyful song and dance on the stage in the pub, nor would there be laughing and talking with his friends afterwards as he and Mason drank and Cass and Orion ate dinner.

He thought back to the day that Mason had first mentioned the lack of the supply plane. That day, they'd sort of brushed it off. They'd gone back to talking about lesser things; Leo regaled a story about the cat he'd found when he lived with Alexander the pianist, he'd invited Mason and Cass around to catch up properly, Orion had teased him about his disorganised pen collection in that dry brand of humour he had (Orion wouldn't say things like that to him now. Orion had hugged him in silence that morning).

Yesterday he'd tried everything he could to get in contact with Hatsumi, or anyone on Earth for that matter, but had ultimately wasted his time. He followed Felix from a distance to try and catch just a hint of conversation, but the steward hadn't spoken a word. In a last-resort effort to find out anything at all, he had dragged himself to Jonah's door and knocked so many times he lost count, but was never honoured with an answer.

Now he knocked on somebody else's door and patiently awaited a response.

As he'd hoped, he was soon greeted with Mason. She wore her usual black shirt and white crossover tie, but without the jacket on top. Something about the look told Leo that she was feeing the same way he was.

"Mason… I'd say 'good morning', but…"

"Bad morning?"

"Bad morning." Leo nodded, "…Did you manage to find out anything last night?"

"Not a thing. But I did see Jonah out of his den for once."

"You saw him? Where?"

"On his way down to the basement, it looked like, with Felix. They were down there for quite a while." Mason paused to fold her arms and lean on the door frame, "I think it's highly likely they're leaving. For whatever reason, I don't know, but if I have to draw a conclusion from what we've seen and heard, that's what I think."

Leo had to admit this seemed a sensible conclusion. In fact, he'd be surprised if Jonah and Felix *did* stick around for longer than today. If he were to force himself to think positively, he would say that they were on their way back to Earth to clarify things with GASO and get the supply plane up to the Exodus as soon as possible, resolving the entire situation. But he wasn't thinking positively, he was thinking realistically. In all likelihood, the captain and his steward were probably leaving everybody else to pay the price of not having enough of the essentials to last them more than a week, with none of the repercussions on themselves.

Even if they didn't need to eat, Leo and Mason still both had people to take care of. The thought of having to watch his friends fade away made Leo feel all empty inside. As much as he wanted to cling onto any sort of life-ring of hope, maybe Orion was right; they really didn't have time to learn to swim.

"Mason…" he began, solemnly, clasping his hands behind his back, "There's something I need to say."

Seeming to sense his risen sobriety in a rare display of reading the room, Mason gave him her undivided attention.

"It's probably too late now, but I just have to say *something*. Or else I fear I'll never get it off my chest. If… If this is our last day of semi-normality before everything goes south for good, I just wanted you to know-"

But before he could finish, a booming bell-like tone rang through the Exodus, the noise bouncing off every surface, rattling the air.

Leo reeled around, shooting his sights towards the speakers on the walls where the sound had exploded from.

Behind him, Cass stumbled to the door to ask what was going on. It wouldn't be long before she got her answer.

A feminine synthesized voice rang out over the speakers, blaringly loud but with such a calm, flat tone.

"Warning. This is not a drill. The emergency auto-destruct system has been activated."

Leo heard the sound of Orion scrambling outside, along with the commotion of people downstairs rushing out onto the concourse to see what was going on, but his eyes stared into the middle distance and his legs were glued in place.

"This station will detonate in T minus fifteen minutes. The detonation override will expire in T minus ten minutes. Please follow evacuation

protocol to ensure the safety of everybody on-board."

And that was when the sirens started. A great gut-wrenching, wailing clamour that seemed to fill the air so violently it felt impossible to catch a breath.

Downstairs, people vied to get to the elevator and piled inside like sardines, and up on the mezzanine those still waking up sprinted out of the door in sleepwear, bags of essentials swinging from their arms as they ran.

With a thud, Leo was knocked by somebody hurrying past, snapping him out of his stupor. He didn't look to see who it was, but swung around to face his friends.

"They won't be able to get into the escape pods…" Orion said, breath staggering as he ran his hands over his face. He stood there in sweatpants and an oversized t-shirt, entirely unprepared. Even his feet were only covered with socks on the cold floor.

If only, Orion thought; if only he had paid more attention to the numbers Felix had revealed to him...

"We need those codes," Leo noted with urgency, "Where can we shut off the self-destruct?"

"Jonah's office?" Mason suggested.

"We'll go there."

"You go to the office, I'll get the codes," Orion told them, definitively.

"You're sure?"

He nodded in certainty.

"I'm not going to play us out as the ship sinks. I'm building a raft."

Chapter 18

The doors to Commander Jonah's cabin crashed open and the figures of two androids stumbled through.

With their combined force, Leo and Mason had managed to break through the double doors into the opulent lair. The precious few minutes spent gaining entrance were not moments they had the privilege of freely wasting, however.

While Leo regained his balance, Mason had already made a beeline to the office and swung open the door in a bid to make up for lost time. The many screens – all channelling bright red – beamed down upon her as she slid into the huge leather executive chair, and on the right wall, a set of panels had folded out to reveal a confusing array of buttons and switches.

Mason wasn't exactly sure how she was supposed to stop the process, and had assumed until now that upon sitting in the chair she would discover a large green button labelled 'stop the ship blowing up'. No such button revealed itself. The screen dead ahead of her in the centre of all the others displayed the countdown timer in minutes, seconds and milliseconds. Underneath was the text 'terminate procedure' and a small box labelled 'authorisation code' awaiting input.

"I didn't expect there to be a code for the termination…"

"Aren't there any instructions? Something to do with all these buttons?" Leo asked, raising his voice to be heard above the wailing sirens as he scanned his eyes over the panels in the wall.

"There will be, but I need a password to get to them," Mason replied. She had no idea what Jonah could have used as a password, she knew so little about him, so she resorted to looking around the office for any hints.

"A password? Why would there be a password?" Leo snapped, "Shouldn't the protocol be available for everybody to access? In case of an emergency? How has he even done that?"

"I don't know!" Mason shot back, "He probably programmed it himself."

"Well, there has to be a way we can find out the password. Maybe it's written down somewhere. I'll have a look around."

"Somehow I don't get the impression Jonah is the type of man to leave confidential information like that just lying around."

"Maybe it's connected to the passcode for the escape pods," Leo suggested.

"Which we don't know."

"But Orion will be with us soon, we just have to do what we can until then..."

The Exodus' basement swarmed with bodies like flies. In the panic of the moment, all order was thrown out the window, and people shoved and clamoured around, making a commotion surprisingly large for a relatively small group.

At the doorway to the pod room, Orion stood on his toes to see past the crowd and identify where the particularly loud, angry voices were coming from.

There, at the front of the mob, stood Felix, besieged by furious figures demanding to be let into the pods. Behind him, Jonah stood in the doorway to his own capsule, trying to pry his steward away from the enclosing throng.

Orion recognised some in particular in the crowd. Doctor Griffin, Mr Dupont the café manager, Paulo the bartender, Tomas (who was currently pouring salt in the wound, shouting out cutting remarks about how none of this would have happened if everybody had just listened to him in the first place), even the Exodus' oldest occupant, Mrs Minsky, hobbled around the outer edges of the gaggle with her walking stick. People who were usually so reserved and tranquil now brimming with vitriol.

If they had any chance of stopping the self-destruct sequence, they had to stop Jonah leaving in that pod. With his own life in danger, it was only logical that the commander would terminate the process. That's if there was a way of turning it off at all.

"Everyone, quiet down!"

Cass' voice resonated around the room, impressively loud to still be heard above the sirens and the arguing. The sheer volume at such a close range made Orion's heart jitter a second. The room fell quiet.

"We still have a chance," she continued, quieter now, when she had obtained the attention of the majority of the group, "If we work together. Right now, Mason and Leo are upstairs working on stopping the auto-destruct as we speak."

This seemed to catch Jonah's attention and his line of sight snapped straight in Cass and Orion's direction, eyes burning with fire. Without a word, he stepped out of the doorway and slammed the door behind him, grabbing Felix by an arm and dragging him through the crowd, knocking Orion's shoulder as they passed.

"...Was that a mistake?"

"No. No, Cass, this is good," Orion said as he watched Jonah stomp down the hall, Felix in tow, "We need to stall him for as long as we can. We should get back to the others."

Despite their accelerated pace, Cass and Orion reached the elevator seconds too late and were forced to restlessly await its return. Impatiently, Cass tapped her foot and chewed at her nails while Orion paced around in circles, staring at the floor.

He'd gone through this kind of thing so many times in his dreams the whole situation made his brain feel fuzzy. If he didn't know better – and he did know better, at least he was pretty certain – he would have thought he was sleeping right now.

Even the siren was starting to sound like the noise of an alarm clock. But he knew that twists like that only happened in stories.

"Orion?"

Torn out of his thoughts, he looked up at last to Cass, who gazed back at him with a mixture of sternness and unease on her face. The elevator doors slid open behind her.

"Let's go, yeah?"

"I'm coming," Orion nodded, and followed her into the lift. Neither of them spoke on their way to the top floor; and when the doors scraped open once again, they made for Jonah's quarters like greyhounds.

When they stumbled through the door, they saw that Jonah had already made a start on wrestling the controls back, grappling with Mason's hands whilst Leo attempted to hold him back from behind. Felix, on the other hand, had his head clasped in his hands, eyes set on the wall clock, as he clenched and unclenched his other two hands in a panicked frenzy.

"*Felix!* The password! Tell us the password!" Leo yelled back to him over his shoulder. But before he could get a reply, Jonah shouted over him.

"Felix, get over here!"

As Felix was about to inch closer, Orion grabbed him by the two right arms and yanked him back. Fighting control against Jonah was already bad enough considering the man's height and stature, they couldn't afford to have another person on his side.

"Hey, let go of me! *Let me go!*" Felix squirmed in Orion's grip, attempting to writhe free, but Cass got hold of his other arms before he could break loose.

There came a crashing thud as Mason pushed back against Jonah in a last-ditch attempt to get him off her, and the chair fell to the floor, bringing the both of them plus Leo with it.

Mason was the first to wobble to her feet again, now free. Her attention turned immediately back to the monitor where the computer still awaited input. She and Leo had already tried everything they could think of. One more incorrect guess and they'd be locked out.

"Warning. The detonation override will expire in T minus five minutes."

The update from the loudspeaker only increased the sense of dread that was steadily building.

Mason shot a look back over her shoulder to Felix. Whether or not the group would survive was almost entirely down to his cooperation.

Mason didn't notice Jonah's hand behind her raising to strike. But the next thing she registered was being jolted out of the way abruptly and the loud thud as Leo crumpled to the ground.

Abandoning her station by the computer, Mason swept down to assist him, dropping to her knees by his side. Above them, Jonah hissed out a

breath between his teeth and shook his stinging
hand, knuckles beginning to bleed.

"I don't have time for this. Felix, we're
leaving."

"Not before you come clean." Cass
tightened her grasp on Felix's arms, "You don't get
to just walk away now."

But to her surprise, Orion released his grip.

"Forget it, Cass. He won't help us, just get
to the computer."

With the timer still rolling down, she didn't
have much of a choice. Leaping over Leo's
sprawled out legs, Cass was quickly back at the
monitor. And soon enough, Orion was positioned
beside her, watching over her shoulder.

"Felix," Jonah warned, reaching out his
skinned hand, "Come on."

Felix looked back at him, now free of all
restraints. The lens of his eye grew larger as he
zoomed in his vision, silent for a few seconds. He
raised his voice above the sirens.

"No, sir. I'm afraid I can't do that."

Jonah let his arm fall to his side. A reddish
mix of disbelief and resentment coloured his face.
He soon shook it off with a loud, angry snort and
reeled backwards before jabbing a finger at Felix.

"If you want to burn up here with the
others, so be it. But don't think for a second I'm
going to wait for you if you change your mind," he
snapped. With that, he turned about and departed
down the hall with forceful steps.

Felix turned back into the room, eye still wide open.

"Cass. TINDERWOOD2033, all capitals. That's the password. Quickly!"

Without waiting another second, Cass typed in the password. But even after she pressed 'enter', she didn't have the time to catch her breath.

"Mason... Mason..."

On the floor, Leo was slowly coming to, reaching out his hand to grasp at Mason's shirt.

"I'm here," she told him, "What is it?"

"Are we safe yet?"

His voice sounded broken-up like an eight-bit synth, the way it sounded after he'd strained too hard onstage, and the right side of his face was crumpled in around his eye and cheek like a crushed tin can. One eye was messed up beyond functioning but he still managed to look up at her with the one he could still move.

"Not yet, Leo. Just hold on."

Mason's eyes caught sight of the screen, where a series of symbols was shown.

Another automated voice rang out with instruction.

'Input the given combination on the secondary control panel.'

"This is gonna take *way* too long!" Cass wailed.

"You read them out, I'll type them in."

Orion had already crossed over to the console in the wall.

"Orion, I don't know what half of these are called. There's no way."

"Describe them. You're creative, you'll think of something. We don't have time to stand around arguing about it."

Cass knew there wasn't really another option.

"Okay," she nodded.

"Ready when you are."

"OK, the first one's like… a really sharp capital E."

"Got it. Next."

"Then there's… two letter S'es, joined up vertically…"

While they worked together to key in the correct combination, Felix steadied himself on the wall, face clasped in his hands. He turned to Mason with a wide stare,

"I can't believe I did that."

She looked up to him from where she sat on the floor with Leo's injured head resting on her knee.

"I couldn't tell you while Jonah was still here. He doesn't know I know the password," Felix went on, "He would have knitted my wiring into a scarf and had my CPU for a paperweight if he'd found out. But I knew it, I found it written behind a picture frame while he slept. I would have spoken up sooner, but…"

"Detonation override will expire in T-minus one minute."

"I was scared, Mason. Now it might be too late. Do you think I'm a coward for what I've done?"

"It's not the time for questions like that, Felix," Mason told him, straight-faced, "Help Orion and Cass."

He almost stumbled over to the console, as a tremendous thudding noise shook the Exodus. The sound of rocket engines could be heard quickly fading into the nothingness.

"*Mon coeur*- what was that?" Leo grimaced, gripping onto Mason's sleeve.

"I believe it was Jonah leaving. Don't worry about it."

His eyes closed in what seemed like relief and his hand fell back by his side but the corners of his mouth still bent down.

Mason recalled the times when she would have to calm young Cass by distracting her. It wasn't something that came naturally to her, but she had done her best to take up the reins after Sam's death by emulating her.

"What do you want to do when we get home, Leo?"

She could see the processors whirring in his head (literally so, if his injury had been slightly more severe) as he formulated a response, but nothing came of it.

"Leo?"

Mason was met only with silence. Reluctantly, she let him rest.

"It's like a... a tall line with three other lines going through it!" Cass called, flapping her hands.

"A- what?"

"I don't know! Like two 'E's back-to-back."

Orion thumbed in what he could only hope was the right key.

"How many more?"

"Two, I think."

As if on cue, the countdown chimed in once more.

"Detonation override will expire in T-minus twenty seconds."

Cass gave a worried whine of pain, sweat pouring down her face. She didn't even take a second to wipe her brow.

"Next there's… a flag with no bottom line. Like a Z at an odd angle stuck to a pole."

"Cass, I'm starting to regret giving you this job-"

"Just find the button, OK?"

"Seventeen," the solemn voice counted.

Orion's eyes scanned the panels in front of him. There had to be at least fifty keys, all higgledy-piggledy and nonsensical in their placement.

To make matters worse, the blood pumping through his veins so hard was starting to make his vision blur.

Shakily, he ran his fingertips along the keys as if it would help him feel out the correct one.

"Fifteen."

"Got it," he announced, slamming the button with conviction, "Next."

"It's a… uh…" Cass' eyes distorted the screen, vision doubling and sliding around. She covered one eye with her hand to regain a small amount of focus.

"Thirteen."

She didn't quite know how to describe the shape. It didn't look like much at all.

Felix leaned in over her shoulder to take a look for himself and memorise the symbol he saw.

"Twelve. Eleven."

"I can't do anything if you don't give me a description, Cass, what are you waiting for?" Orion snapped, hands trembling over the keypad.

"Ten."

"It's like- like a square with two pairs of arms flexing and one is upside-down, or two 'C's that got impaled if you look at the negative space, like something from those old ancient jugs."

"Nine."

"Ancient jugs? Cass, this makes *no* sense."

"Eight."

"Like a motif, it could make a larger pattern."

"Seven. Six."

Orion looked once more for anything fitting the description, but nothing stood out, and his sight was getting worse. The calm manner in which the voice counted downwards to his death added to his mounting irritability.

"Five. Four."

"Just press anything! Anything!" Cass yelped, tears starting to stream down her face as her heart dropped further into her chest.

"Three."

Felix tripped over to stand beside Orion and steadied himself holding onto the lower panel of the wall.

"Two."

Felix's eye snapped to one specific button. One segment of a Greek key pattern that somewhat fit Cass' description. The last thing he wanted was to make a mistake at the last hurdle. But Orion was still stalling.

"One."

Felix's hand smacked down upon the key and all fell silent.

Orion looked down at him with icy blue, piercing eyes, and even Cass turned about to look at them as she caught her breath.

"Orion… I'm so sorry. I was just trying to-"

"Detonation overridden. Self-destruct protocol de-activating."

Orion choked out something half way between a laugh and a sigh of relief and the next thing Felix knew, he was being squeezed half to death.

"Felix, you lifesaver, you actually did it-" Orion pulled away for a second before Cass pulled both him and Felix into a group hug.

"I- I think you'll find I only pressed one button," Felix murmured awkwardly as Cass flung her arm around his shoulders.

"Teamwork! Teamwork!" She grinned, rocking side to side in excitement, "Mason, Leo, we did it! We-…"

As she reeled around to look to her two other friends, she noticed their situation at last. Her smile melted from her face and her arms dropped back to her sides as she slowly approached Mason and Leo, crouching down by their side.

Mason was silent, focused on picking broken pieces of metal from the crumpled mess of Leo's face.

"Leo?" Cass started, "We're safe now, we did it. Did you hear?"

But still there came no reply, not even after prompting from Orion.

"I think the connection to his power supply is ripped," Mason said.

"Well can you fix it?" Orion asked, having crashed down from the rush of success back to reality all at once.

Mason clenched her teeth together, examining the extent of the damage. The repairs she had previously carried out at work were usually minor – a disconnected hand at worst – but this was a whole new kettle of fish. Not only would she have to reconnect the power supply, but she would have to piece back together the remnants of face and check for more damages.

"I can *try,*" she said, eventually.

"You're good at this sort of thing, right? He'll be okay?"

"I'll do everything I can, Orion."

Adrenaline levels dropping at last, Orion breathed a heavy sigh and finally slumped over to relax. Whatever happened, he knew Leo was in the best hands he possibly could be. And for now, they were alive.

Chapter 19

The sounds of quiet chatter bubbled in the air, coupled with the soft purr of machinery. The incidental squeak of a small wheel seemed almost piercingly loud against the accompanying noises.

Slowly, Leo opened his eyes.

A bright light glared down at him like a big, square, glowing eye against the dark ceiling of the basement workshop.

Leo pulled together the power to shift to a sitting position, and as soon as he began to move, the chatter dissolved.

"Leo…"

His vision swiftly calibrated and he was met with the familiar face of Mason seated across from him on a wheeled stool, hair tucked behind her ears. Beside her was a metal trolley cluttered with odds and ends, cuttings and scraps. At the back of it all stood a soldering iron, propped up in a neat little stand, a tub of flux, and what remained of Leo's gold-rimmed glasses.

Orion's voice, from somewhere behind, spoke his name in a breathy, relieved tone, and Leo could hear him get to his feet at once.

"Good afternoon, Leo," Mason said, calmly. Her hands were folded neatly in her lap and her face was somewhat reassuringly deadpan.

"Good… afternoon," he repeated after her.

The last thing he remembered was the blaring sirens… the grey walls of Jonah's office…

the distorted, wavy vision. Everything had seemed to run in a weird, jittery slow-motion.

"We thought we'd lost you for a while."

"What happened?" Leo asked, accepting the risk of sounding cliché.

"Well. The ship didn't explode."

"You really did it, then... I knew you could. I'm sorry to have missed it."

"Actually, you have the others to thank for being here right now. With Orion's quick planning, Cass' creativity and Felix's mettle, we got out of there by the skin of our teeth."

"Felix?" Leo turned about to see the three on the other side of the room. Cass and Felix were seated on wooden crates, and Orion stood beside them, watching with concern, "You're still here?"

"Where else would I be?" Felix responded. He sat almost as if he didn't belong, like a juvenile troublemaker brought in to the local police station for questioning.

"I thought you left with Jonah?"

"You must have been more out of it than I thought," Orion said, "Felix was with us the whole time. He pressed the final button. Didn't you, Felix?"

Felix nodded in silence, clearly reluctant to truly take pride in his actions.

"It was nothing."

"Are you kidding?" Cass scoffed, "Those last moments were so tense I almost got a hernia.

I've been trying to chill out for the last few hours
to get over it."

"Hours?" Leo repeated.

"Yeah, you've been out like a light.
Probably 'cause your face was all smashed in.
Mason fixed it up, though."

"I did what I could," Mason put in. She
bent down to pick up a mirror from the trolley and,
when Leo looked back to her expectantly, held it
up for him, "I'm afraid it's not without blemish.
The damage was a little deeper than I anticipated. I
don't think I could have survived a hit like that."

Leo gazed into the mirror to assess his face.
A long, raised seam ran from the centre of his
forehead and snaked down like a stream to the
underneath of his right cheekbone, stitched
together with red thread. The slight colour
difference between either side of the seam
indicated to Leo that the 'skin' he bore on the right
was not originally his own. Most likely something
found in the dark recesses of Mason's many
shelves and drawers.

"The suture is just there while the glue
sets," she went on, "I can't promise it won't leave
a permanent mark."

Leo looked up to her as he ran his fingers
over the seam, and cracked a bashful smile.

"We *match…*"

"I suppose we do," Mason smiled back at
him, lowering the mirror. From the look on his
face, Leo wasn't particularly bothered by the

whole thing – in fact, he looked almost happy about it.

"If you decide you want something neater, you can always ask Hatsumi when you see him again."

"...We're going home?"

"Felix got the communications open again," Mason nodded, "There's a transport plane on its way, but it might take a day or two."

Leo's face brightened further and he sat up straight at last.

"My things- I should get my things together!"

"Orion will take care of that," Mason reprimanded, "You just focus on rest and recalibration, alright?"

"Okay." Leo gave a soft grin, "Doctor's orders?"

"Doctor's orders."

"Mostly everyone else is already back in their rooms getting their stuff packed away or just trying to relax," Cass said, "They weren't much help at the end of the day, but I hear they tried their best to stop uncle Jonah leaving, so there's that."

"And where is he now?"

"Out in the escape pod flying through space somewhere." Cass shrugged.

"I thought you'd be more concerned."

She lifted her feet up onto the crate and wrapped her arms around her legs, resting her chin on her knees. With a sort of sad air, she pursed her lips.

"I don't really know what I think about uncle Jonah any more," she said, "I used to think he was just hard at work looking out for us, but, y'know… the whole 'burn up here with the others' thing kinda put a dampener on it."

"Sorry, Cass."

"Eh, don't worry about it. I'll figure it out. I guess it's good to know the truth. My last living relative is a depraved monster and we're left to pick up the pieces. Too bad, huh?"

"You always have us."

She puffed out a grateful laugh and the corners of her mouth turned up once more.

"Guess I do."

"What was his deal, anyway?" Orion asked the whole room, "We never got an answer out of him."

"I believe only Felix knows," Mason replied.

All eyes turned onto the timid, four-armed android in the corner.

Felix shifted his weight, nervously, all four of his hands looking out-of-place wherever he put them.

"Nobody's going to be angry with you, Felix," Leo assured him, "Just tell us what happened."

"Well…" Felix began, averting his eye to the floor, "It's a long story. It goes back about a decade. Mr-… I mean, Jonah, wasn't happy that Levi hadn't given him a senior role in GASO, or that he never got credit for anything the organisation did. Whatever news outlets covered GASO and Ruhigdorf only ever gave merit to Levi. That's how it all started, anyway. Then it sort of snowballed. He brewed in his anger until it bubbled over. I suppose he thought that if he couldn't have the glory, neither could his brother." Felix crossed his arms and raised his gaze to look at the others at last, "The fire was only supposed to target Levi's house. He bribed Kay O'Donnell to pull it off for him. To wreck all that Levi had worked for. It wasn't really supposed to kill him, or anyone for that matter.

After the fire burnt near everything in the house, he went in and claimed his spoils of war from the fireproof boxes. And after the deed was done, all he wanted to do was take Levi's place in GASO and bask in the wealth he'd accrued, but there was a whole village of people left without homes getting in the way. He didn't want to take everyone up to the Exodus – he didn't want to leave Earth at all – but he decided that it would negate suspicion. So here we are."

"And you just stood by and watched it happen?"

"Orion…" Mason warned, "Leave it."

"There was nothing I could do," Felix went on, "And believe me, I tried. But whenever I attempted to speak up, he'd tell me he'd have me deactivated. I'm a coward, Orion. I couldn't stop anything. Once we were all up here, things seemed to be going OK. And they were, for a while. Up until the new 'rumours' started. Tomas started figuring it out. Jonah got nervous. He'd still been clinging onto the belief that Ruhigdorf would be fully rebuilt soon and that he could go back home and get back to normality, and nobody would be any the wiser. The last thing he wanted was people figuring him out."

"So if Tomas had stayed quiet…"

"None of this would have happened. For better or for worse. When his theory gained more traction, Jonah's plan was to starve out the Exodus and then jump ship at the last minute and tell everyone down at GASO that it was their fault for not sending up supplies in time after 'missing' a message that he had never really sent out. But then people started to catch on and, well, that plan went out of the window. You know the rest. I'm sorry I didn't do anything sooner. I couldn't bear to leave in the pod with Jonah and leave you all there. I knew I was the only one who could help you. That's why I stayed. I don't want anything to do with that good-for-nothing wolf any more. I've always admired the way you four friends care for each-other. I wish I could have been a part of it."

The room fell silent.

Cass stared dead ahead, still processing the mountain of information that had been dropped upon her, while Mason sat looking typically nonplussed.

As if looking for an indicator on what to do next, Leo turned his head from Felix to Mason, but didn't receive much in the way of advice.

"Thank you for being valiant when we needed you," Mason said, eventually, "That's what counts, I believe."

Felix flashed a small smile that soon disappeared again as he wrapped his arms around himself and let his gaze settle in the middle distance.

"I should probably be going," he said with a sober inflexion, "I think I need to rest for a while."

"I'll walk you upstairs," Orion said.

"Oh- that's very kind of you, but-"

"I insist."

"Well… only since you insist."

Felix got to his feet and trailed after Orion out of the workshop, closing the door meekly behind him.

In the returning silence, Leo once again turned his attention to Mason with a regretful air.

"I'm sorry I didn't help much when it came to it."

"Nonsense." Mason brushed his remark off like dust, "I think you may have saved my life. Jumping in front of Jonah like that – that takes courage. I admire your bravery."

Somewhat taken aback, Leo ran a hand through his hair and neatly crossed his legs.

"Why, thank you. I admire your…" He paused as he thought of the best possible response to this compliment, "…Altruism."

And if she could have done, Mason might have blushed.

*

"Felix."

Felix stopped dead in his tracks. He had thought that he had managed to avoid conversation with Orion for the entire trip upstairs, but as they both exited the lift, his hope of going home in silence began to crumble. He turned around almost in slow-motion.

"Yes, Orion?"

"I think I was wrong about you," Orion said. His face didn't smile, but his eyes were gentle and calm, "You're not a bad guy. You just got stuck in a bad situation. I'm sorry for treating you like dirt. As dramatic as it sounds, you saved all our lives back there in Jonah's office while I just stalled. So I suppose I just wanted to say… thanks. For not just leaving me to die. And, uh, sorry for calling you 'camera boy'."

Felix made the closest thing to a laugh that Orion had ever heard come out of his mouth and a wide smile spread across his face.

"I understand, Orion. Consider yourself forgiven."

"Thank you, Felix... I don't see any reason why our little group doesn't have room for one more."

"A-Are you sure?"

"Of course."

"Well. I don't know what to say. And you're certain the others won't mind?"

"Very certain. Why don't you come by my room later and we can play some chess?"

"That sounds… That sounds *delightful*."

"Good. I'll see you later, then, Felix?"

Felix nodded his head, gratefully,

"And I'll see you too."

With a pat on the shoulder, Orion bid him farewell, and Felix turned to leave. And the android's trademark gait seemed less like a worried jog and more like a cheerful skip as he went.

<u>Epilogue</u>

Cass had forgotten the warmth of the sun on her skin.

Despite the fact that it was October, the day that the rescue plane reached Earth was surprisingly sunny. Or perhaps it just felt that way.

The journey from the Exodus had taken around a day and a half, but had felt so much longer. Maybe it was anticipation, or maybe just plain boredom, that had made the flight seem to drag. But now the occupants had their feet placed firmly on solid ground, they hardly knew where to start.

Cass raised a hand to shield her eyes from the sun, leaving one of the two suitcases she was pulling behind her to lean on her leg.

From up on top of the moor, the modest village of Ruhigdorf sat ahead of her, quietly nestled in the loving embrace of the surrounding trees. To the west, the chimneys and dormers of the old Goldschmidt house were just about visible over the rooftops of the other buildings before it. Cass saw the Copper Cedar pub, with its white brick walls and black shale roof. And she was sure that, if he was looking, Orion would be able to see his old home in amongst the others.

Cass turned around to see if he was looking at all, but he seemed pre-occupied. He walked alongside Felix, engrossed in a story, trailing his suitcase behind him.

Just a little way behind them, Leo and Mason followed suit, Leo's arm linked through his friend's for stability. Undeterred by his injuries (including a more recently discovered mildly warped leg), he had insisted he wanted to walk the two miles into Ruhigdorf from the runway. Though Cass would have probably preferred to take the provided coach transport, they had decided to take a shortcut over the moors, walking the dirt path through the tall grass. The trail was quite in stark contrast from walking the shiny modern halls of the Exodus for the past four years.

Years.

It was hard to believe it had been that long. When up on the station, Cass had felt like it was the only place she'd ever been, and now she was down on Earth again, it felt as if she'd never left.

She came to the sudden realisation that it had been years since she had seen an animal.

Quickly, her eyes scouted the horizon for any fluffy white sheep, but to her dismay, she found none. But as she carried on down the path, a jackdaw landed with a flutter on a signpost just ahead. It cawed a couple of times, then turned its head to look straight at her.

Cass stopped in her tracks to watch it a while, and eventually Mason and Leo came to stand on her right, and Felix and Orion on her left.

"What's wrong?" Mason asked.

"Nothing. Just watching the bird…" Cass breathed in a half-whisper, "It's been a while since I last saw a bird."

With that, the jackdaw departed, leaving behind a single black feather which slowly floated to the ground to rest in-amongst the heather.

"Come on, we're almost there," Mason said, relieving Cass of a suitcase, "Just down this slope."

They made their way down the side of the small hillock, dirt crunching underfoot, until they reached the village and were welcomed by its quaint old bounds.

They'd approached from the rear, the Goldschmidt house and forest to the west, and the square to the east.

Everybody else who had departed the plane had opted to take the provided transport back home, and would be taking the longer route around to approach from the north. With how far removed the place was from the nearest town or city, the long empty road seemed to curve away over the horizon into nothingness. Soon the coach would roll up and park up at the Goldschmidt house (though now a sign reading 'The Old Manor Hotel' stood proudly at the end of its driveway), but until then, it was just Cass and her quintet of friends.

They turned right when they met the road, to the square, just to see. In the centre of the square there was a small green encircled by flowerbeds where a dogwood tree used to stand. It had died in the fire, and now in its place was a young sapling. And tending to the sapling, watering can in hand, was an old gentleman with an impressively mechanically-complex prosthetic leg.

"Hatsumi?"

He stood up straight and turned around at the sound of Leo's voice.

"Leo, my *son*."

Leo let go of Mason's arm and half-limped, half-lurched over to Hatsumi, where the scientist wrapped him in his arms. And when they parted again, Hatsumi laid his hands on Leo's shoulders and inspected his face. More specifically, he regarded the new scar.

"Very precise… I must assume this is Mason's handiwork?"

"That's right, all improvised from spare materials, too," Leo told him, with a proud lilt to his voice.

"I would expect no less. Well done, Mason," Hatsumi smiled, holding his hand out to Mason, who by this time had moved with the others to stand around him. She shook his hand, formally.

"Thank you, doctor. It means a lot coming from you."

He flippantly waved his other hand at her as if to brush off a thought,

"Please, no formalities, Hatsumi will do fine. It's bad enough having Leo here refer to me by my family name, despite our history. It's good to see you again."

"You too, Doctor Hatsumi."

"Oh, and young Cass…" He gripped her hand in that way that old men do, with a sure firmness despite the slight shake in the wrist, "How you've grown since we last spoke."

Cass had to admit it had been a long time. They hadn't really had a proper conversation before, and all she knew about him was whatever Leo had told her and the snippets she could remember her father telling her. From the way her father spoke of him, she could tell that Hatsumi had been a sort of mentor to him, at least in the earlier years of his career. She hadn't seen his face in a long time, either. He had sleepy, gentle eyes and his wrinkles were deep set in his face like the bark of an old tree. His smile was framed by a grey handlebar moustache and short, square patch of beard on his chin, the hair on his head neatly combed and gelled, not a hair out of place. A man of meticulous detail, Cass could tell.

In turn, Hatsumi greeted both Orion and Felix, complimenting them and the rest of the group on the initiative they had displayed in the crisis days before.

"I am glad that you're all home safe," he said, clasping his hands together, "I don't think this village could have taken another tragedy… I regret that I wasn't able to assist at all, I think I owe you all an apology for not realising that something was wrong.”

“No; no apology necessary, you weren’t to know,” Mason assured him, “And even if you did, I’m not sure the situation would have ended any differently if Jonah had discovered that he’d been… found out.”

“Perhaps you’re right, Mason. In any case, you’re home now. I think it’s time you five relaxed.”

“But what about Jonah?” Felix piped up.

“All will be taken care of in due time. Rest assured it’s out of your hands now, Felix.”

Hatsumi paused to look back over his shoulder to the green and to the humble shops surrounding the square with a certain fondness in his eyes.

“I would have met you at the landing strip, but… Well, I thought I had better make sure everything was perfect to welcome everybody back,” he said, gently, “I have some things to finish yet. If you head over to the manor I will meet you and the coach there shortly to discuss housing arrangements so we can get you settled in as soon as possible. If you would..?”

“Of course, we’ll see you soon.” Mason turned to walk away, with the others following close behind her, all trawling their cases behind them.

But as they were leaving, Leo came to a halt at the back of the group. Slowly, he turned about until he was facing his inventor once more, and patiently waited until his friends were just out of earshot.

"Hatsumi."

He put his arms behind his back and shifted his weight on his feet for a second.

"When I called you from the Exodus… the last time we spoke. I asked you whether androids had the capacity for love. Like people."

"I remember."

"Well... I got my answer." Leo gave a brief smile before he stepped away, "That's all."

ෂℭ

www.ingramcontent.com/pod-product-compliance
Lightning Source LLC
Chambersburg PA
CBHW061344160726
47995CB00001B/169